Chronicles OF GABRIEL

USA Today Bestselling Author

W.J. MAY

Copyright 2022 by W.J. May

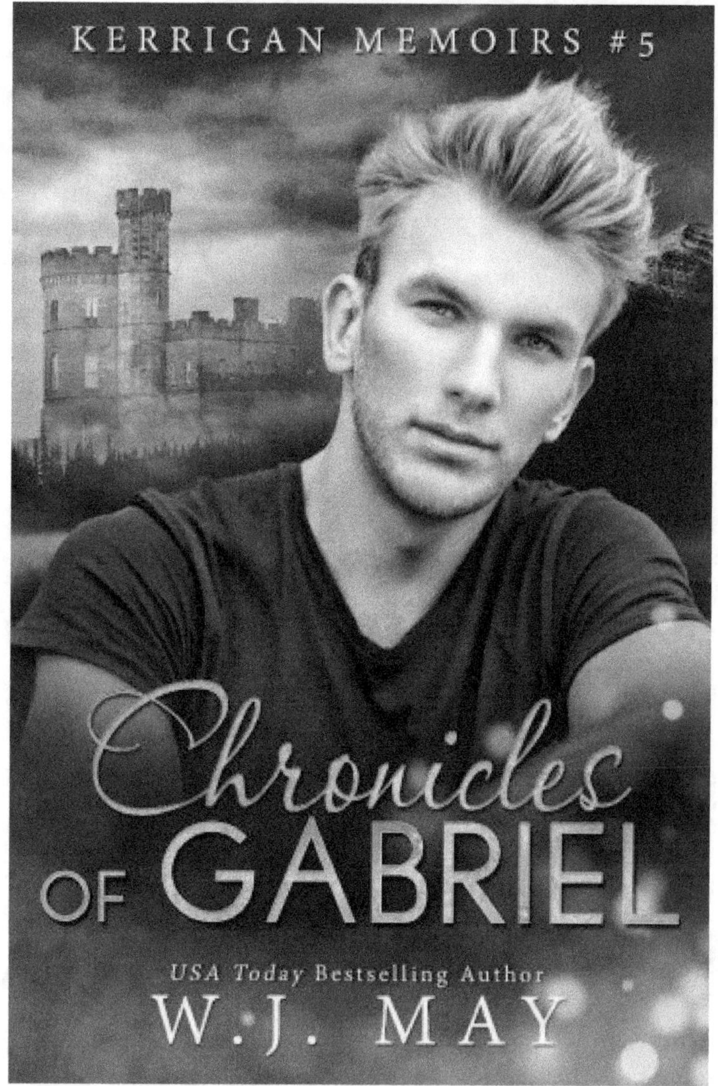

KERRIGAN MEMOIRS #5
Chronicles
OF GABRIEL
USA Today Bestselling Author
W.J. MAY

Chronicles of Gabriel

Kerrigan Memoirs, Volume 5

W.J. May

Published by Dark Shadow Publishing, 2022.

CHRONICLES OF GABRIEL

First edition. September 15, 2022.

Written by W.J. May.

WAIT – Guess What's Coming?

Author note: I have loved writing Gabriel's story so much, I am going to come back to the Kerrigan Kids, along with Gabriel and Devon as part of the storyline!!

Stay tuned for more details...

Kerrigan Memoirs Series

The Chronicles of:
Devon
Angel
Julian
Molly
Gabriel
Rae

Have You Read the C.o.K Series?

The Prequel series is a Sub-Series of the Chronicles of Kerrigan.
The prequel on how Simon Kerrigan met Beth!!
Download for FREE:

THE CHRONICLES OF KERRIGAN: PREQUEL –
Christmas Before the Magic
Question the Darkness
Into the Darkness
Fight the Darkness
Alone in the Darkness
Lost the Darkness

THE CHRONICLES OF KERRIGAN

Book I - *Rae of Hope* is FREE!
Book Trailer:
http://www.youtube.com/watch?v=gILAwXxx8MU
Book II - *Dark Nebula*
Book Trailer:
http://www.youtube.com/watch?v=Ca24STi_bFM
Book III - *House of Cards*
Book IV - *Royal Tea*
Book V - *Under Fire*
Book VI - *End in Sight*
Book VII – *Hidden Darkness*
Book VIII – *Twisted Together*
Book IX – *Mark of Fate*
Book X – *Strength & Power*
Book XI – *Last One Standing*
Book XII – *Rae of Light*

THE CHRONICLES OF KERRIGAN SEQUEL

Matter of Time
Time Piece
Second Chance
Glitch in Time
Our Time
Precious Time

The Chronicles of Kerrigan: Gabriel

*L*earn about Gabriel's story, if you haven't already read it!

Living in the Past

Present for Today

Staring at the Future

Kerrigan Chronicles

Book 1 – Stopping Time
Book 2 – A Passage of Time
Book 3 – Ticking Clock
Book 4 – Just in Time
Book 5 – Time in the City
Book 6 – Ultimate Future

The Kerrigan Kids Series

Book 1 - School of Potential
Book 2 - Myths & Magic
Book 3 - Kith & Kin
Book 4 - Playing With Power
Book 5 - Line of Ancestry
Book 6 - Descent of Hope
Book 7 – Illusion of Shadows
Book 8 – Frozen by the Future
Book 9 – Guilt of My Past
Book 10 – Demise of Magic

Book 11- Rise of the Prophecy
Book 12 – Deafened by the Past

Find W.J. May

Website:

https://www.wjmaybooks.com

Facebook:

https://www.facebook.com/pages/Author-WJ-May-FAN-PAGE/
141170442608149

Newsletter:

SIGN UP FOR W.J. May's Newsletter to find out about new releases, updates, cover reveals and even freebies!

http://www.wjmaybooks.com/subscribe

Chronicles of Gabriel

GABRIEL ALDEN WAS LIVING the fairytale... after a nightmare.

He'd replaced his childhood ghosts with a lovably neurotic family. The shadows that chased him were finally laid to rest. He'd adopted a son and was about to marry the girl of his dreams.

So why did he keep waiting for the other shoe to drop? Probably because it always does.

After a prison break from the heart of the Privy Council, the supernatural community is shaken to its core. Despite Carter's insistence that everything is business as usual, agents are still being targeted, Barnes' forces are growing, and it's impossible to know who to trust.

In the days leading up to his wedding, Gabriel finds himself questioning all kinds of things he'd believed to be certain. Can a person with his history make a decent father? Can he learn to operate within the same ethical boundaries as the others? Will his compass ever point true north, or will it always be a little skewed?

Sometimes happily ever after is only the beginning...

Chapter 1

Gabriel Alden stood rigid as a statue, staring at the man in front of him.

His muscles were tense and his hands were ready, but the rest of him was strangely calm. He had been in this situation before. Many, many times. This was familiar territory.

Come on...blink.

The security had been dismissed, and the room was empty, save for the long counter in between them. No cameras, witnesses. Upon that counter, lay upwards of fifty million pounds.

The man was sweating. The air conditioner was turned up to full blast.

"Is that really how you want to answer?" Gabriel asked softly.

Unlike the rest of the people in the building, he'd brought no weapons. Even the trusty blade he carried in the hollow of his shoe had been left beside the bed. Of course, he didn't need to bring weapons. He didn't need anything other than his bare hands. But there was no need to advertise that now.

Anytime...blink.

The man swallowed hard, but stood his ground.

He'd probably been in this situation almost as many times as Gabriel. He was also at an advantage. He was only the intermediary for the arrangement. The terms of the exchange had already been set.

"I'm afraid"—he caught himself at the look in the assassin's eye—"I'm afraid there's nothing more that can be done. We have reached the end of my purview. The decision is not mine to make."

Really.

Gabriel's lips curved, and the temperature jumped another ten degrees. "Your hands are tied, there's nothing more than can be done." His gaze deepened, holding the man in perfect suspension. "Can't tell you how many times I've heard that."

The clock struck high noon. The man flinched.

"I suppose I could make a call..."

Victory.

Gabriel held out his hand with a genuine smile. "Give me the diamond."

The tension shattered as the man reached behind the glass, carefully extracting a velvet cushion topped with a trio of glittering bands. Two of them were immediately set back amongst the others while he offered the third between them, cupping it gently in a pair of gloved hands.

"Are you sure, sir? You wouldn't prefer the sapphire?"

Gabriel stared for a brief moment, holding it to the light.

"Best to keep things matching, George. But I appreciate the consideration." He slipped it into his pocket and pulled out a card. "And don't bother with the call. I'm happy to pay full price."

The man paused in surprise, already reaching for his mobile. "Are you certain, Mr. Alden? You seemed quite—"

"I just like to play with you, George." Gabriel smiled again, fiddling obsessively with the ring as the man rang him up. "Keeps the blood flowing, doesn't it?"

There was a cheerful *ding*, and the card was passed back to him.

"We should do this more often, sir."

The two men shook hands, then went their separate ways. One vanished into the storeroom for a strong hit of espresso followed by an Ambien, while the other strode into the sunlight, fishing the ring from his pocket and balancing the glittering diamonds in the palm of his hand.

Only the once...

HAVANA WAS SWELTERING that time of year, but Gabriel decided to walk—peeling off his English blazer and blending into the rest of the locals with nothing but a white tee shirt and jeans. It was still early, not even noon, but the streets were already sizzling with coquitos and jasmine.

He walked straight up the center of the road, driving back the scooters and motorcycles with a wave of pedestrians. The first time he'd come to Cuba, he'd been nine years old. Cromfield had been incredibly strict thus far in allowing him to leave the country, but he'd been learning Spanish for the last two years and there was allegedly a conjurer living on the island. When the jet had flown, he'd flown along with it. Then they'd landed...and he'd spent the entire visit on the beach.

It was unprecedented, what had happened. Utterly surreal. He didn't have anything to compare it to. For the first time, he was simply not needed. The mission had enough lookouts and guards, his tatù hadn't yet manifested, and he wasn't even tall enough to bind the prisoner's arms.

He was dismissed. And he loved every second of it.

So many times he'd replayed the memory, he could recite every frame. The way the air had smelled of salted mangos and suntan oil. The way the sand had felt between his toes. He hadn't even gone into the water, didn't get that far. He was still making his way towards it when one of the drivers had been sent to get him. The man felt so sorry, they'd stopped for tacos on the way back.

Maybe we could forget an English wedding and do the whole thing here. Fly over a little group of people, have everyone walk down to the beach. Natasha wouldn't mind, she's never been to Havana...

His face stilled with a wistful smile. Then he thought it a little further.

Limited extradition, with an untested catering staff. Molly wouldn't like that.

He thought a little more.

...Angel would.

He turned away from the beach and lifted his hand to the street. They were in a quieter part of town, but a winding frontage road stretched the length of the island. A taxi stopped in seconds.

"Sí, señor?"

He saw the brim of a hat, the flash of a smile. "Aeropuerto, por favor."

The car took off as he slid across the leather, if not for a handy bit of magic, he wouldn't have been able to shut the door in time. His gaze drifted with a smile over the seat to the driver. His head bobbed along to nonexistent music. One hand was permanently embedded in a bag of chips.

Yeah, Natasha would love this...

His eyes clouded at the same time.

...but I'm not sure about Jason.

It was a phrase he'd been looping a lot more often, the closer they drew to the big day. All the progress the two had been making, all those little steps that Gabriel had built to mountains in his mind...it was like they were in a chapter belonging to someone else. Despite having bonded, despite having lived almost two full years together, the two were suddenly brand new in each other's eyes.

It wasn't the same with Natasha. She and Jason were close as they'd ever been.

"You flying back to London?"

Gabriel flashed a look towards the driver, catching his eyes in the rearview mirror. "See, I spoke to you in Spanish. What makes you question me in English? For all you know, I could be from here. I look exactly the same as everyone else wandering that beach."

He knew this for a fact. He had studied relentlessly just to make sure. And yet, it had taken the man all of about two seconds to peg him as English. A cursory glance, between crisps.

The driver chuckled, swerving dangerously close to a scooter. "You mean besides your pasty English face?"

He means your golden radiance.

"Plenty of guys like that on the island." Gabriel tilted his head with a grin, aware he'd already lost the argument several blocks back. "I'm serious...what gives me away?"

It was one of the things he liked most about the country—none of his tricks seemed to work quite as well as anywhere else. People had a scent for authenticity. The man who'd picked him up when he landed had been the same way. So was the old woman who'd cooked him dinner.

"It's your walk."

Gabriel leaned forward with interest. "My walk?"

The man nodded, his eyes glued to the road. "You walk like you have somewhere to be. Around these parts, people get to places when they're good and ready. There is no...no pressing need for it. You also wear a watch."

There was a pause.

"I don't wear a watch."

"Your walk implies one."

Fair enough.

Gabriel's eyes drifted out the window, absently counting the industrial buildings as they passed by. It had been three days he'd been on the island, and ironically enough, there hadn't been some pressing place for him to be. He'd been wandering the streets like everyone else, breathing in the salted air, drinking rum and basking in the sunsets. It was almost like a vacation.

"Actually, could you pull over here for a minute?"

The driver glanced back in surprise before steering them onto the curb. Gabriel jumped out, but purposely left his jacket, calling over his shoulder as he jogged across the street.

"Thanks, I'll just be a sec."

Most of the buildings on the edge of the city were refineries of some kind. Many were for sugar, others processed and packaged pharmaceuticals. A few of them even housed the small planes that drug-runners used to get on and off the island. But those were of little concern to Gabriel. He'd come there for a specific purpose. Apparently, that purpose had leaked into his walk.

He leapt the chain-link fence and cooed at the guard dogs, tossing them the remains of his breakfast as he jogged briskly around to the opposite side of the building. There were large windows on every floor, but they were calcified to the point of losing all functionality.

He swept right past them, knocking twice, before pulling open the door.

Four men glanced up immediately, seated around the same card game. Four guns were propped beside them. They blinked in astonishment as he flashed them a bright smile.

"Sorry to interrupt. Is one of you guys Cal?"

They stared a split second, then pointed in unison to a man in the middle. Gabriel flicked his fingers and each of their guns lifted into the air, firing four rounds straight into Cal's chest.

"Perfect—thanks!"

A chorus of shouts erupted behind him as the others staggered away from the table and sprang to their feet. They reached for their weapons, only to find them floating almost tauntingly towards the ceiling. They rounded on the golden-haired assassin a second later, only to glimpse him already jogging back towards the street. The dogs licked at his shoes when he passed.

He hopped the fence, then deliberately slowed his gait to something less hurried, looking quite pleased with himself for the effort. At the same time, the table collapsed and a cloud of blood-splattered playing cards fluttered slowly to the ground. Only then did they discover his parting gift.

He'd slapped a plastic explosive to the door.

Three...two...one...

The building exploded with enough force to quake the street, but enough directed precision to harm only the people still cursing inside. Gabriel dusted off his jeans as the fireball curled into the sky above him, blotting out that beautiful sunshine with a cloud of acrid black smoke.

It had already cleared by the time he rounded the corner and crossed the street, slipping into the idling taxi. The driver turned around slowly, and Gabriel flashed him another cheerful smile.

"*Now*...let's head to the airport."

GABRIEL DIDN'T STOP at the main terminal when they reached the airstrip, but directed the cab towards a group of private planes on the other side. Two of them bore governmental insignias, but the others were conspicuously absent of identifying markers. A few of their pilots were idling beside them, scrolling through celebrity gossip and blowing clouds of cigarette smoke into the balmy day.

The cab rolled to a stop.

"This is you?" the driver asked in surprise.

He'd driven wealthy Englishmen before—and no matter how proud this one seemed of his carefully-selected sandals, he was clearly a wealthy Englishmen—but never anything like this.

Gabriel glanced out the window, reaching into his pocket. "I'm a personal shopper." He passed a card through the grate, rolling his eyes towards the shiny row of planes. "You wouldn't believe some of the nonsense these people think up."

The man's eyes twinkled as he passed back a receipt. "I wouldn't be surprised..."

Gabriel stared a split second, then flashed a parting smile and stepped onto the tarmac, casually reactivating the GPS locater with a twitch of his hand. The taxi sped off towards the exit while he slung a bag over his shoulder and jogged up the descending stairwell of the nearest plane.

There was no need to guess *which* plane. It was the only one without a tail number.

A blast of air conditioning struck him the second he set foot inside, shivering over his sun-washed skin and making him reach for the discarded blazer. It slipped back over his arms as he gave a quick nod to the pilot and headed down the narrow hallway into the main cabin.

A frazzled case officer was already inside, clutching a cellphone to his ear.

"And I understand that—" He waved a silent greeting to Gabriel, trying his best to interrupt the angry tirade coming from the other side of the Atlantic. "Richard, I understand—" He broke off again, rubbing at his temples. "Well sure, that's one interpretation—"

A string of choice profanities echoed through the phone, getting steadily louder with each one. The man drew in a breath, then covered the receiver with a strained smile.

"I'm sorry, Alden. This will just take a second."

Gabriel lifted his hands, settling in the seat across from him.

It wasn't the first time he'd been shelved for a more urgent problem. The man doing the shelving wasn't even supposed to be sitting on the plane. He was a field-office manager, accustomed to sitting in a London suburb somewhere, answering phones. But those lines had started to blur after Cliff Barnes broke open the cells beneath the PC and took almost half the agency with him.

Agents had been left without partners. Caseloads had started doubling up.

The only good thing that could be said about the supernatural exodus, was that it had been relatively peaceful. But in a way, that wasn't surprising. This hadn't been a professional squabble, but a rift in the heart of a community. The people who left weren't just names on a sheet of paper.

They were friends.

"No, Richard. I can't *make* him transform..."

The engine had started when Gabriel locked eyes with the pilot and the plane was already taxiing onto the runway. The Privy Council didn't generally adhere to the idea of *taking turns*, the same way they staunchly refused to file a flight plan. Somewhere amidst the slew of governmental connections and magical assists, its agents had grown accustomed to the finer things in life. On most flights, a heavily-tailored attendant would have already offered a drink. No such person appeared.

"—can't just rent out another submersible, there is a *weight* limit to these things. Now if you insist upon diving with the—" An angry pause. Much more shouting. *"Then put Roger on the line!"*

There was an odd grinding sound and the case officer lowered the phone briefly from his ear, holding it like a prayer to his chest. There had already been an impressive number of calls that morning. And no matter the shifting time-zone, it always seemed to be ten o'clock.

Gabriel regarded him with a touch of sympathy, then took advantage of the lull.

"I got him," he whispered.

The man covered the receiver. "What?"

"The bad guy, I got him."

The case officer rolled his eyes with a grin. And a migraine. There was an empty clipboard sitting on his lap. One they weren't technically supposed to take off without completing.

He tossed it from his legs onto Gabriel's.

"Draw me a picture."

With a flash of mischief, the assassin leaned back in his chair and proceeded to do just that—transforming the case summary into a flowering garden, adding gradually to the latitude and longitude, until if anyone checked, the mission would have occurred somewhere close to the moon.

He'd just put the final touches on a pair of disgruntled seals, when he caught the man's eye twitch and caged them with an obedient smile, scribbling down answers to the same questions he'd been asked a thousand times before. Did you need to kill so many people? Should you have killed more people? Are there some people out there, *right now*, that we should be tracking down to kill?

Not for the first time, he wondered how his friends answered the same questions.

He doubted they were asked of Molly, while Luke was probably required to fill them out in cuneiform on a rock. Julian likely left his case reports blank, unless he knew that someone in the future was going to read them, while he suspected that Devon had found a way to imprint each one upon his very soul. Rae would probably be drawing seals just like he was.

Angel would give the seals guns.

He finished with the clipboard and reached into his pocket, tracing the tips of his fingers around the diamond band. It was delicate, just like the engagement ring he'd purchased what felt like only a few blinks before. The day was racing towards them, groaning beneath the weight of a million nonsensical logistics, but it still couldn't come fast enough. This was his *wedding*. To *Natasha*.

He would have married her yesterday. He would marry her tomorrow.

He would marry her the second he got home.

"—freeze the iguana—"

His eyes lifted slowly, drifting across the tiny cabin and settling on the case officer's face. By the looks of things, the conversation had deteriorated quickly. It had also taken a bit of a turn.

"I can't get anyone there until at least tomorrow," the man muttered, pulling another phone from his pocket and scrolling frantically down the screen. "I just picked up Alden in Havana and we're heading back to Heathrow. But we'll be passing close enough that I could—"

"I'll do it."

Three conversations in two different time zones, came to a pause. The case officer stared across the cabin without blinking, tiny drops of sweat trickling down the sides of his face.

"...you will?"

"Why not?" Gabriel tossed back the clipboard with a smile, raking his fingers through his wavy hair. "We're all finished here. It'll give me a chance to stretch my legs."

In the blink of an eye, things were set into motion. Plans shifted and new coordinates were given to the pilot. A fresh batch of phone calls were made to a corporation somewhere in Germany, and in a tiny office building in North Carolina, an aged secretary went racing down the hall.

"Thank you," the case officer murmured, leaning back into his chair with a wan smile. It was too early to say for sure, but there was a good chance he was going to live an extra five years. "Shall I have them send over the file? There isn't much time before landing, but—"

"Just give me a location. I'll figure it out inside."

The ring was tucked safely back into his pocket, as Gabriel's heart quickened with a rush of adrenaline. For a passing moment, it felt almost like the old days.

No restrictions. No predictability. No net. Just point him in the right direction and let nature take its course. It was absolute freedom. And never had he found something at which he so excelled.

A part of him almost missed it.

Another part was trying very hard to forget.

Chapter 2

The plane touched down just after dusk, sinking into the tall grasses of a Savannah skyline.

Gabriel could hear the cicadas before the wheels even finished turning, a sweeping chorus that rushed inside his ears, like shells getting dragged back to the sea. The air was sharp, yet sweet with the scent of palmettos mixed with honey. And *humid*, he'd forgotten how humid it was in the American South. A warm breeze swept down the second the door that had opened, curling his waves into tendrils and sticking his tee shirt to the front of his chest.

Good thing I came from Cuba.

"Good thing you came from Cuba," the case officer echoed his thoughts, peeking just enough of his head out the door to squint into the setting sun. "You're already dressed for it."

Once he'd been freed from that strangling panic, *Kevin* had actually turned out to be a lovely companion. A little star-struck, but that could no longer be avoided. More than anything, he was simply grateful. He and the others had been stretched just as thin as the agents were themselves.

Gabriel nodded mutely, his vision narrowing to the target. "And we think the place is deserted?"

There had been a failed recovery attempt, this much he had learned from the man on the plane. Bad intel, from the sounds of it. The enemy had been alerted, and the target was no longer inside. But an agent was still trapped there, having walked into a situation that was sure to get a few dozen underlings fired. The reason for this was unknown. Perhaps injury, perhaps worse. The radio link had gone dead a few hours earlier. For all they knew, the agent was already in the ground.

Kevin glanced back at his phone, re-reading the latest updates at the speed of light.

They might have been in a pastoral field, but the man's ink stretched a bit past that, projecting so high into the atmosphere above them, it allowed him to act as a virtual satellite.

"That's what they're assuming—nothing but the hotel staff and our man inside." He paused ever so slightly, tensing at the same time. "There's a good chance it's a collection, not a rescue."

Gabriel nodded again, it was nothing more than he expected.

They rescued the agents. They collected the bodies.

This guy's already been off the grid a long time.

"Don't wait up."

Kevin nodded automatically, then caught himself just as fast.

"Wait—*don't* wait up?" he repeated anxiously.

Far be it from him to disagree with the famed assassin, but at the same time, he didn't want to be the man responsible for the death of Gabriel Alden. Especially this close to his wedding.

Especially this close to his friends.

"What if you need backup?" he argued before Gabriel could answer. "What if something goes wrong, and you need a quick getaway, or just—"

"And you have time for that?" Gabriel answered with a light smile, turning back long enough to snap a fresh round of ammunition into place. "Be honest, where were you heading next?"

There was a pause, followed by a reluctant mumble.

"Prisoner transfer. This fallen oligarch in Bucharest—"

"Go—do that," Gabriel interrupted, turning back to the road. "I'll be fine here. And I'll be finding a way back for myself."

The man started nodding, then grimaced instead. "And what if...?"

Their eyes met.

"I know how to transport a body."

There was another pause, then the two shook hands.

It was a rather dour note to end on, but time was of the essence, and these days, situations rarely allowed for anything more. Barnes may not have attacked them directly, but he'd left them high and dry. If the other side didn't get them, there was a strong case to be made for friendly fire.

The engine thrummed to life and the plane streaked across the ground behind him as Gabriel made his way with the greatest of caution through trees.

Despite the fact that they weren't far from civilization, there was something utterly wild about the feel of it. Like walking through an old time novel, where the pages cracked beneath your fingers and everyone had frogs in their backyards. He stepped lightly, on guard for any sound that didn't fit in with the landscape. The snap of metal, the rubber creak of a shoe. Free from the usual constraints of a city, his ink was able to fan out and perform a function it was rarely allowed: search.

So often it was used merely for destruction—whether that be deflecting a bullet, collapsing a building, or holding a person hostage using nothing but their own blood. It seemed he never played anymore with the nuance—the bits he focused on when he was learning. The elemental variation in the things around them, the tiny complexities as things could be merged and parted in distinct ways.

It was science, what he did. Wizard's science, maybe. But science nonetheless.

He'd told this to Natasha once in a moment of drunken clarity. He was a scientist—nay, the world's *greatest* scientist. He'd gotten a sarcastic coffee mug to that effect the following day.

But there was nothing. No weapons, no trip wires. No static hum of radios wedged in unfriendly ears. Only the soft call of a summer swallow as the sun dipped below the trees. The hotel appeared a few minutes later—framed like a fairytale upon the crest of a moonlit hill.

Just like the brochure had said.

He eased out of the underbrush and stepped onto the gravel driveway, shrugging off the mossy branches of the towering oaks. At a closer look, there was nothing particularly fairytale about it. Or Southern, for that matter. Instead of being the overpriced antebellum reenactment he'd been expecting, the place looked like it had sprung right from the pages of a detective novel.

Probably a few secret passageways. Probably a few false doors.

Definitely haunted.

And from the look of things...it was actually deserted.

He slowed down ever so slightly, trying to determine the best way inside.

As much as he'd come to admire certain aspects of the Privy Council, both he and Angel still preferred to do their own reconnaissance whenever possible. When the office worker on the plane had claimed the action was already over, he'd prepared to go in, guns blazing, just in case. But unless the enemy had approached on foot like him—a terrible strategy for a direct assault—then it was quite possible Kevin was right. There were only two cars in the parking lot, and one of them hadn't run in over a century. The other was a passenger vehicle—almost impossible to armor, and slower than almost everything that might come up against it on the road. They might have stormed the hotel and successfully relocated their asset, but they had left sometime earlier that day.

So he's either strapped to a chair with a bag over his head, or they buried him beneath these lovely trees.

Gabriel threw a reflexive glance over his shoulder, unsure which he would prefer.

Short of any better ideas, he threw caution to the wind and jogged lightly up the wooden steps, nodding politely to the doorman as he passed by. The man was armed, but with something better suited for squirrels. He also wasn't nearly as shaken as he ought to be.

The lobby was a different story. Whatever happened in the lobby had to have hurt.

There weren't many parts that weren't soaked through in blood, and all of them had been left to the tired attendance of an elderly janitor—a man who'd decided to combat the problem with a single bucket of water and an undervalued mop. Gabriel paused immediately upon entering, then picked his way carefully across the tiles, pausing a bit uncertainly when he reached the front desk.

What the hell is happening...?

"Good evening, sir."

Gabriel froze where he stood, half-expecting a pair of cursed twins to wander down the stairs and barter for his soul. Here was another misfitting piece of the puzzle. Another character straight out of *Sherlock Holmes.* The man was posed with an imperious expression between a crystal vase and landline telephone that was actually so old, it was dial up. Hand to the heart, he lowered a monocle before he spoke.

"Are you interested in booking a room?"

Is this some kind of movie set? Is everyone who works here a ghost?

Gabriel swallowed hard and took a step closer, forcing his lips into a strained approximation of a smile. Truth be told, he had no idea how to respond. They were standing in the middle of an *actual* bloodbath. The man had an unblemished handkerchief tucked into his lapel.

When in doubt, a simple approach was often best.

"Actually, I'm looking for a friend of mine."

Gabriel's mind blanked in shock, as he abruptly realized he'd never actually asked for the missing agent's name. Or his tatù. Or a physical description. All those pesky little details.

Blame the case officer. Never look back.

"He's, uh...he's traveling alone. Might be kind of tall...?"

"You're talking about Mr. Delaway, sir," the man answered with the greatest of authority, taking the lens from his eye and polishing it with gloved hands. "He flew in a few days ago, and I'm afraid his business here didn't go as he'd planned. He has retired into the southern wing."

Gabriel lifted his eyebrows in surprise. "...he has?"

Is that euphemistic?

The man nodded gravely.

"I didn't have the heart to refuse him. Such a charming young fellow, despite his troubles. After the gunfire was over, he asked if he could please relocate to my study and bleed out in peace."

There was a pause.

"He said it like that?" Gabriel repeated with sudden interest. "He said please?"

The man nodded, and he glanced towards the stairs with a grin.

Julian.

"YOU OVER-MANNERED FOP."

There was a sudden movement on one of the chairs beside the fire, and a set of dark eyes peered over the top. Julian sprang to his feet a second later, framed by two stuffed pheasants.

"It's you!" he cried in dismay. "*You're* who they sent?"

Gabriel took a step inside. "You're welcome."

This room didn't give off the same homicidal vibes as the other. The lights were dim, the air smelled of bourbon, and the entire length of the walls were covered in leather-bound books. Despite the balmy evening, a cheerful fire cracked in the hearth, adding a soft, golden glow to the ambiance.

That being said, a generous helping of blood had been smeared across the floor, and most of it had pooled around the recliner where his friend had been sitting. A rather troublesome image, but Julian appeared alert and focused. At the very least, he was certainly feeling free to speak his mind.

"I was hoping for Sonders or Boyd," he continued in exasperation, either not realizing or not caring that he was being incredibly rude. "They're both in Germany, just a quick flight—"

"You got me," Gabriel interrupted, taking a step closer.

With a practiced eye, he assessed his friend again—searching for any details he might have missed. Given the amount of blood they were dealing with, it was unlikely at least some of it didn't belong to Julian. He wanted very much to examine him properly, from a closer distance, but his friends had recently made it quite clear they were tired of his attempts to 'play doctor.'

He'd begged them to call it something different. They'd refused.

"I'm fine," Julian said preemptively, as if guessing he might try. "Just a few grazing bullets, already cauterized. Don't let this little house of horrors fool you."

On that note...

"I was just in the lobby," Gabriel said sternly, folding his arms with a shrewd stare. "Did you do something unkind?"

Julian smiled humorlessly, taking a revolver from his jacket pocket. "I can't take all the credit. They were the ones who decided to fight back."

Gabriel laughed quietly, watching as he reloaded the clip. "I was starting to think you guys booked some kind of murder-mystery for my bachelor party," he confessed. "And I couldn't imagine why you'd think I would like something like that."

"No, that's all been settled." The psychic lifted his head slowly, leveling his brother-in-law with a hard stare. "And I'm *not* telling you what it is."

Getting into the ancient spirit of these things, Gabriel had tried to bully the information out of him several times before. Not because he particularly cared what the psychic was planning, but because he discovered that he liked the act of bullying *immensely*. On the flip side of the coin, Julian had been left with the unsettling realization that he was a *little* bit frightened of his new brother.

The smile lingered as Gabriel glanced around the stately shelves.

"Still, it's a nice place you tore up."

Julian shrugged, typing something into his phone. "I guess."

Unlike the rest of their friends, who'd received an English inheritance or grown up in New York's Upper East Side, both Gabriel and Julian had experienced a different side of life. While they more than made up for it now, the psychic wasn't often impressed by money. The last time they'd gone to the palace, Julian had spent most of the time downloading apps onto his phone.

Gabriel circled around slowly, the firelight dancing in his eyes. "It's almost unsettling," he murmured, pausing to examine a magnifying glass. "The kind of place where they drink julips, murder immigrants, and take shots of Teddy Roosevelt's blood."

The psychic cursed under his breath. "Damnit."

"What?"

"You just guessed *exactly* what we're doing for your bachelor party."

Gabriel flashed a grin, rejoining him by the fire.

It might have been one of the more bizarre situations he'd found himself in that month, but if Julian didn't seem worried, he wasn't going to worry himself. That being said, the psychic *was* in the process of arming himself, and there were still a few details they needed to get straight.

"So they ambushed you?" he asked abruptly, casting a look out the window. "They took the thing you were...whatever it was you were looking for?"

Julian glanced up from his phone. "Sorry?"

Gabriel flushed, but pressed forward. "You know...the thing. You weren't able to find it?"

For the first time, the psychic warmed with a true smile.

"The *thing*," he repeated slowly. "You didn't read the case file, did you?"

There was an incriminating silence, then Gabriel threw up his hands.

"Okay, first off—"

Julian laughed loudly, shaking his head. "Getting sloppy, Alden. I've seen first year recruits who are more prepared."

"*First* off," Gabriel interrupted angrily, "I'm sorry for not briefing myself on *your* mission, Decker. Some of us were out there solving problems of our own. And *second*, you're lucky that I even showed up to save your ass. If we hadn't been flying by—"

"Sincerest apologies. Thank you for saving me."

"—bloody right," the assassin concluded in a huff. "I took a detour all the way to the wrong *Georgia*, only to find you already blew the mission, and *this* is the gratitude I get. It's unacceptable."

"You're my hero."

Julian slung a bag over his shoulder, flashing a quick look to the future. "And I didn't blow the mission," he added abruptly, those prophetic swirls already darkening to the present. "I found the safe they sent me after."

Gabriel glanced up in surprise. "...what?"

"The safe. It's here."

What?

"Still?"

"Still."

"So the concierge—"

"—is in on it."

"And the rest of the men?"

"Mercenaries hired out of Fort Wayne last week." Julian cast another glance out the window, tying back his hair. "They should get back here any minute."

There was an incredulous pause.

"So you really *did* want Sonders and Boyd."

"I hate those guys," Julian answered, heading to the door. "And there's a decent chance we're about to get killed." He clapped him on the arm with a smile. "It's good to see you, though."

Gabriel stared at the back of his head, fighting back the urge to laugh.

People often mistook Julian's quiet wisdom for pragmatism, or even worse, they felt he was inherently grounded. But the man was none of those things. One could argue, he was actually a bit unstable. Unstable enough for Angela Cross to have fallen in love with.

"You coming?"

Gabriel headed after him with a grin.

That's all right. We've never been accused of being sane.

Chapter 3

The bullets started flying the second they opened the door.

They cratered into the walls on either side, echoed by an explosion of wooden splinters and the sharp scent of pine. Most were loose-handed shots, but a few of them struck a little too close for comfort. Gabriel's ear was sliced almost immediately. Julian jerked backwards with a gasp. For the space of a single heartbeat, they were too stunned to move. Then they came to and dove for cover.

Gabriel threw up his hands as they landed, deflecting whatever bullets were still airborne and sending them right back the way they'd come. There was a pair of screams, the sound of reloading.

"Why are they so angry?" He panted. "You didn't even take their little safe."

Julian slumped against the wall beside him. "They probably guessed that I wanted it." He grimaced and extracted a long wooden splinter from his arm. "I kind of shouted as much when I was killing their men."

Gabriel shot him a sideways glance, then nodded. "Yeah, that was probably it."

Another shower of bullets struck the wall beside them.

"So what's the plan, princess?" Gabriel tried to ease around the corner for a better angle, only to whip back just as fast. "I'm assuming you have one, and while it might not be the best time to admit it, there's a chance I actually *didn't* read the case file."

Silence.

"Jules?"

He glanced over his shoulder, only to see the psychic in a clairvoyant trance. Streams of white light poured from his eyes while his fingers were still gripped around his weapon.

That's not safe.

"Perfect timing," he muttered under his breath. "Like going to battle with a narcoleptic."

Another hailstorm of debris rained down upon them, and he ducked his head. Truth be told, he hadn't counted on doubling his number of opponents, but he'd come through worse odds.

"That's okay, I'll just do it myself."

He pressed his back flat against the wall, abandoning the idea of conventional weapons, and deciding to use his ink instead. There was a good chance the men were wearing inhibitors, given that Julian hadn't seen them coming, but there was still plenty of metal in the room around them, and he'd never been deterred by the idea of property damage like perhaps he should.

He lifted his hands, feeling the telltale sizzle on his arm. But a second before he could leap into the open, a sudden hand curled around his jacket—slamming him back into the wall.

"Not yet."

Normally, there wasn't a thing in the world that could cut through the adrenaline, but a few short words from the psychic did the trick. Julian knelt on the tile in front of him, dark eyes dilated in concentration, then, in a flash of speed he stretched his arm around the corner and fired six shots.

He did this without looking. Six targets fell to the ground.

...that works.

Gabriel pushed slowly to his feet, staring at the back of the psychic's head. He was already reloading his gun, slipping briefly into the future to make sure the stairwell was clear.

"Alright...you can date my sister. I'll allow you to date Angel."

Julian flashed a grin. "That's nice of you."

Yes, it is.

Together, the two men raced down the hallway and towards the stairs.

There were a few more unwelcome surprises, a few more close calls they would inevitably revisit later that night as they tried to fall asleep. Whoever the men were, they had come prepared, each of them draped in a blinking inhibitor. They had also come angry—still smarting from being so thoroughly trounced by a single man, and relishing the chance to finish off the psychic for good.

They hadn't counted on his temper. Nor on the arrival of his friend.

"Heads up!"

Gabriel shifted momentum on a dime, half-tackling Julian from the scope of a sniper. They tumbled into the wall at the same time, winded and gasping for breath, but he'd already peeked out from behind the corner—dislodging a chandelier with a flick of his hand and sending it like a clattering ghost upon their attackers. It scooped two of them into the air, shaking them violently, before casting them straight through the open window. There was a distant shout, then silence.

Julian picked himself up slowly, staring with wide eyes. "You took *Beauty and the Beast way* too seriously."

Gabriel caught him by the sleeve, racing forward once again. "You're the one who told me to watch the classics."

They darted down the stairwell and towards the front doors, picking off gunmen one after another, before leaping over the final piece of railing and somersaulting across the foyer. The marble tiles were still sopping with blood—a detail they noticed while peeling themselves off the ground.

"Crap," Julian muttered in disgust, flinging drops from his hands. "It's in my mouth."

"That's what you get for leaving a *mess*, Julian," Gabriel chided, wiping his face with the back of his hands. There was movement somewhere above them, but the immediate coast was clear. "So where's this safe? You said it was still on the premises?"

An uncharacteristic flush darkened the psychic's cheeks. "Yeah, it's...it's upstairs in the study."

Gabriel turned slowly, and the two of them locked eyes.

Usually his brother-in-law could be counted on to keep a level of composure, but between the flying candlesticks and the fact that he looked like he'd been dipped in Halloween, he broke fairly quickly. The flush deepened as he gestured upstairs, muttering unintelligibly under his breath.

Gabriel pursed his lips, cupping a hand over his ear. "Sorry, what was that?"

Julian let out an irritable sigh.

"I couldn't move it," he repeated. "The thing was supposed to be—*stop laughing, Gabriel*—the thing was supposed to be mounted in the wall, but they sank it into concrete instead. It's still made of metal," he added causally. "So you could just..." He trailed off with a vague wave of his hand.

This is adorable.

Gabriel tilted his head. "I could just...what?"

Julian sighed again, casting another look up the stairs. "You know what."

"I don't," Gabriel argued cheerfully. "I haven't the faintest idea."

"Could you just—" The psychic gestured impatiently towards the ceiling. "They're literally regrouping, you lunatic. Don't make me say it."

"Say what?"

"*Gabriel.*"

"*Julian.*"

There was another pause.

"Could you get the safe?"

Gabriel raised an eyebrow.

"*Please.* Could you please get the safe?"

With another blood-spattered grin, Gabriel lifted a hand—letting his eyes drift out of focus as he scanned quickly through the rest of the hotel. There was nothing but the usual; sinks in the bathroom, frames on the pictures, knobs on the doors. But in *one* room, there was something more.

There was a pain on his arm, like the sting of a burn.

Come on...

The safe might have been three stories up, but he felt each corner as though it was gripped between his hands. His muscles strained and his pulse quickened, a mounting pressure in his chest was making it difficult to breathe. The psychic was right, it was deep in the concrete. Too deep to attempt from such a distance. But his training had never allowed for such constraints.

Only a few seconds later, it broke free.

The sound must have been incredible, but they were too far away to hear. They felt it instead—the thud of the concrete, the wailing screech of each metal bolt. By the time the men racing towards them knew what was happening, it was already flying like a kite down the stairwell, knocking them down like human bowling pins, before skidding to a theatric stop at Gabriel's feet.

"I found the safe," he whispered loudly.

Julian stared a split second, then let out a breath of laughter.

"You're such an arse," he muttered, shaking his head with a grin. "Even when you're helping, you're still one."

Gabriel dipped his hand through the metal, extracting a small camera from inside. "Aw...you think I helped?"

They shared a brief look, then took off running once again.

The lobby might have been sparse before, but amidst the hail of gunfire, it was completely deserted. The doorman was gone. The janitor had run for cover. Even the old car parked beyond the windows, the one Gabriel would have sworn had been forged sometime in the late Jurassic, had been inexplicably coaxed to life and was already rolling down the country road.

...which only left one man.

"Are you checking out already, sir?"

Both men screeched to a sudden stop, staring in shock as the concierge lowered his monocle and picked up an old lantern instead. To be honest, the sight of it was so puzzling, that neither one of them had any idea what was going to happen next. They were too busy staring at the riding gloves and waistcoat. They were too busy wondering why the man was still manning the abandoned desk.

They were still staring when that lantern shattered over their heads.

"Bloody hell," Gabriel cursed, waving his hand hastily between them. The antique telephone lifted into the air, bashing him over the head. "It's like the house that Arthur Conan Doyle built."

"What is that...?" Julian asked in dismay, sniffing at his coat. "Kerosene?"

The glass fragments hadn't been the problem, it was the questionable liquid that followed, seeping into their hair and dousing them from head to toe.

Gabriel peeled off his shirt, tossing it across the floor. "Just be glad it wasn't an inhibitor."

The psychic didn't look like he would be glad about anything. He looked very much like he might never be glad again. But he nodded mutely, following Gabriel outside.

"I might have preferred the inhibitor," he mumbled, shaking out his hair and knotting it messily behind his head. "They're already wearing them. It's not like I could see them..."

Both men froze perfectly still.

"...coming."

The second they'd stepped onto the porch, upwards of fifty armed men stepped forward to meet them. *Heavily* armed men. With the kind of artillery usually reserved for battlefields and military demonstrations. In the blink of an eye, a cloud of tiny red laser dots appeared on their chests.

Gabriel drew in a quick breath, eyes sweeping the grassy lawn.

"Julian...we are never staying in this hotel again."

His brother-in-law was frozen beside him, standing so completely rigid, it was like he could actually feel each of the scopes moving over his skin. Three times, his eyes flashed to the future, but he didn't volunteer any information, and judging by the hard set to his mouth, it didn't look good.

In a strange way, that made their next moves rather simple.

So they're feeling a bit theatric?

Gabriel lifted his hands slowly into the air.

I've been known to be rather theatric myself...

"I surrender," he said plainly. "You've done a fantastic job and we're clearly out of options. I want to personally congratulate each and every one of you."

A whispered hiss rippled through the crowd, and Julian closed his eyes.

"Please don't," he murmured. "I know that look. Whatever you're planning...just don't."

Gabriel flashed a bright smile. "Nonsense. Look, we're already making headway."

An actual tank rumbled out of the trees, getting in line behind all the rest.

"We have the camera you're after," he continued openly. "It's inside my friend's jacket pocket. Unfortunately, we've also been doused in kerosene by your cartoonishly spectacled friend, so I'm afraid if you fire any of those lovely weapons, you might very well destroy it yourselves."

The dots wavered uncertainly, but didn't disappear.

"If someone would be kind enough to toss over a pair of cable ties, we'd be more than happy to bind each other's wrists. Then perhaps we could speak to the person in charge...?"

In the silence that followed, half a dozen pairs of eyes drifted towards a man standing beside the tank. Gabriel's eyes drifted over as well, warming with a little smile.

Gotcha.

It was difficult to describe exactly what happened next—difficult for the people watching, and difficult for the PC case officer who'd read about it in the days to follow, re-reading each line in the quiet of his office with the same puzzled frown.

Instead of using all the metal, of which there was an absurd amount, instead of summoning himself a weapon, which were also in numerous supply, instead of diving for cover, Gabriel closed his eyes—reaching not for what was in front of him, but for what lay deeper.

Reaching for what was buried in the ground.

There was a rumbling deep below them. The earth itself gave a single shudder—like it was drawing in a breath. Then all at once, a literal sandstorm sprang up from the ground, twisting into the air like a creature come to life, and swooping down with violent intensity upon those watching.

Nickel, cobalt, iron, tin.

As many weapons as the enemy had brought, the very ground they were standing on had been seeded with more of the same. The air they breathed had been laced with it. The blood in their veins rose up in protest, curling in on itself in a terrifying clamor of gunfire and screams. They cried out uselessly, batting at the metallic cloud that had engulfed them before all at once, the lovely swatch of Savannah countryside had gone eerily silent and still.

The men were gone, strewn in tangled patterns across the grass. The only thing left standing was the tank, but even that seemed to wilt before them, like it had been left too long in the sun.

Alas...there's no one left to applaud.

Julian was still frozen, standing a half-step behind with his mouth hanging ajar. After a few seconds, when it became clear that no one was getting up, he managed to pull in a breath.

"Okay."

Gabriel flashed him a sideways glance. "Everyone's a critic."

"No, I just..." The psychic took a step forward, staring around in surprise. A full minute passed before he looked back with genuine admiration. "That was *very* nice, Gabriel."

The tension shattered with an unlikely smile.

"Thank you."

"I'm serious," Julian continued. "That was very clever. How did you think of that?"

The two men jogged down the wooden steps and fell into pace alongside each other, picking their way through the chaotic tangle, as they set off walking into the night.

"I was actually thinking about it on the walk over," Gabriel answered lightly. "These things always feel so scripted, but I'm not some blunt instrument, you know? There's an art to it."

Julian nodded thoughtfully. "I can see that."

They paused a moment to regard the tank before setting off down the road.

"I've actually always fancied myself a bit of a scientist..."

Chapter 4

"**J**ules, wake up."

Considering they were just a trans-Atlantic flight away, it hadn't been the easiest trip back to London. After hitchhiking to the nearest truck stop to shower and wash away the blood (arguably the most unsettling part of the mission), the men had booked a cab and grabbed tickets on the last flight leaving for Heathrow, only for the camera they'd discovered to self-detonate in Julian's bag.

It had been a randomized timer, something he hadn't seen coming. But it had blown straight through his personal laptop and gotten him such an enthusiastic pat-down from airport security, it was bound to leave psychological scars. He'd stared in silence at the remains, then petulantly retired the second they'd landed on English soil. He'd been blacked out in the cab ever since.

"Julian," Gabriel murmured again, giving him a gentle shake, "we're almost there."

The psychic blinked open his eyes, staring vacantly out the window.

They'd left in the evening, flown backwards through the night, and landed in London at the crest of a new dawn. The city was just awakening, warm in a glow of pink sunlight. The xenophobic joggers were leaving before they had to risk awkward encounters with their neighbors. The late-night cabbies were smoking. The bakers were setting out fresh loaves of bread.

Another continuation to a never-ending day.

"Did you get any sleep?"

Gabriel shook his head briskly.

The friends liked to joke that his and Angel's training had left them a bit more feral than the others, but the truth was, his body was literally incapable of shutting down until the completion of a mission. For most agents, this meant when the mission itself was over. For agents who'd been raised by a madman beneath a cemetery, this meant when they returned like carrier pigeons to the nest.

"None at all?" Julian leaned forward a little to catch his eye. "You know, Angel's been trying these new breathing techniques that she swears are—"

"Are you still retired?"

Since his return from a particularly gruesome mission in Hungary, the others had started making jokes about the psychic's retirement as well. It had lasted all of about five minutes. The 'five minutes that shook a nation,' as Luke liked to call it. The jokes would last much longer.

Julian rolled his eyes with a grin. "I'm on the fence."

The car bumped over the road—evading the city's meticulously spread new pavement, and managing to find every remaining pothole east of the Thames. Their heads knocked lightly against the window as the sun began to rise above the buildings, piercing the cab with a flash of light.

"How did you get there?" the psychic continued abruptly. "To the hotel, I mean."

"I was on my way home from Cuba, took a detour in the jet." Gabriel cast him a sideways look, thinking back on the deserted parking lot. "What about you? I didn't see anything."

The psychic thought back with a frown, wondering the same thing himself. Not even when they were hiking to the freeway, had the question crossed his mind.

"I rented a Jeep." Julian started to say more, then paused. "...I think it blew up."

Gabriel nodded calmly, searching for his keys. "Did you get the insurance?"

Julian swiveled around to face him, looking very young. "Do *you* get the insurance?"

I never know when they're kidding.

Gabriel leaned back with a grin, having been signing extreme liability waivers since he was thirteen. It was one of the ways he tested his fluency in different languages. He'd memorized words like negligence and disfigurement in Portuguese before almost anything else.

"What did they teach you at that school?"

Julian threw up his hands, unwilling to say the party line. "I'm psychic," he declared instead. "I am the insurance."

"...you didn't see it blowing up?"

In what might later be condemned as a clairvoyant deflection, a prophetic glow swept across Julian's face. A little frown tightened his brow before his eyes cleared with sudden intensity.

"What's that?"

Gabriel went immediately still. "What?"

"That thing you're about to reach for."

"I didn't decide to reach for—" Gabriel caught himself just as quickly, glancing down to see his hand already halfway inside his pocket. His fingers closed around the delicate band, the same way they'd been doing without thinking since he left Havana. "...I didn't realize I was."

Julian waited a moment, but when his friend didn't elaborate, he reached inside the pocket himself—pulling out a little circle of diamonds, then freezing in surprise. "Oh, that wasn't..." He stared a second longer before his eyes lifted with a smile. "You got a ring in Cuba?"

Gabriel nodded, feeling abruptly nervous. "Yeah, you know...somewhere in between the beach volleyball and shaved ice."

Julian smiled again, lifting it towards the light. "No sapphires, huh?"

There had been some debate as to whether Natasha had been passing a 'coded message' in her choice of tiara for the latest ballet, or if they'd all been spending too much time at the theater.

"Just the diamonds," Gabriel replied, watching the tiny refractions of light bounce around the interior of the cab. "George and I thought it was best to keep things matching."

The psychic looked up sharply. "You didn't give him any trouble, did you?"

"None at all."

There was a moment of rendering, then he passed back the ring.

"That's nice...she'll love that."

Gabriel let out a slow breath, feeling his pulse return to normal. "Really?"

It wasn't just that he was eager for an opinion. As a rule, psychics didn't speak lightly. And his brother-in-law's words carried a bit more weight than most.

Julian drifted into the future, then returned with a twinkling smile. "Yeah, she will. Which reminds me, Molly wanted you to call. Something about endangered sheep...?"

A silence fell between them, then Gabriel's face cleared with sudden understanding.

"No, it's this—" He shook his head, waving it off. "It's for the wedding. She's trying to get her hands on this illegal kind of cheese."

Julian cast him a quick look, then nodded without saying anything.

"Cool," he finally managed.

Considering the relative size of London, it was starting to feel like a small town. The family-owned cafés and art-house cinemas each came with a memory, and as they crossed the heart of the city and started moving towards their little corner, a few people actually waved as they drove by.

Gabriel might have lived in the city all his life, but he'd never felt anything like it. There was a sense of community that was completely foreign, one that made him tense instead of smile. One that made him jealous of his easier-going friends, as he always waved back a second too late.

"Thanks for coming," Julian said suddenly. Gabriel glanced up in surprise to see the psychic staring with a strange expression out the window, the lights of the passing buildings flashing in his eyes. "That might have gone a little...I can't see what would have happened if you hadn't come."

There had been several moments when he'd thought it was already over. Several moments when the future slipped from his grasp, and he thought they'd gone too far. Fly close enough to the sun, and even the ancient Greeks had lost their wings. It's why agents weren't typically permitted to fly unless it was with each other. But in the wake of Barnes' departure, those rules had changed.

"Yeah, of course," Gabriel answered softly. They sat there in silence as the taxi pulled into the cul-de-sac, then he flashed a quick smile. "Sorry it wasn't who you wanted."

Julian chuckled and rapped on the glass. "Can you go to mine first, please?" He pointed towards the cottage across the street. "I want to change into different clothes before Angel wakes up. She's merciless about this kind of thing."

It was Gabriel's turn to laugh, though he was hardly dressed any better. There had been few options at the truck stop where they'd done their shopping. That being said, there was a chance the psychic hadn't actually read the *Gimme Some Southern Hospitality* sweatshirt before yanking it off the hanger. The only thing worse were the pair of neon orange sunglasses nestled in his dark hair.

"Angel once got herself stuck in a latex kimono," he replied with a grin. "In case you need a little ammunition."

Julian clapped him on the shoulder. "You're a good man."

He passed the driver some money and stepped onto the pavement—waving over his shoulder, as he started jogging towards the house. Gabriel watched him with a slight frown, feeling unsettled without knowing the reason. It wasn't until he reached the porch that it suddenly clicked.

"Jules," he called out the window, "were you hoping for Sonders and Boyd?"

The psychic nodded curiously. "They're not here anymore. They left."

THE REST OF THE CITY might still have been sleeping, but things started a little earlier at the Alden house. By the time Gabriel unlocked the door and slipped inside, there were voices coming from the kitchen, and the smell of coffee and pancake batter was already drifting through the air.

He ghosted down the hallway, warming with an involuntary smile.

"—sprinkle in a pinch of salt—"

These were always his favorite moments, when he caught his new family unawares.

There was nothing he loved more than to catch a burst of laughter when he turned off the shower, or round the corner only to stumble upon some happy scene. Since the moment they'd laid eyes upon each other, Jason and Natasha had fused with some magical bond. The kind that teemed with shared mischief and secret smiles, the kind that had grown stronger each night she helped him fall asleep when he first arrived, humming quiet lullabies and combing her fingers through his hair.

It was a wild sort of love, and tender at the core. Too big a thing to be contained between the two of them—they spread it messily around. In the weeks, then months that followed, Gabriel had made it his personal mission to be close enough that it spread onto him as well.

"A *pinch*, Jase!" Natasha exclaimed, swatting down his hands. "Keep that up and we'll have to throw this batch away, too. Don't tell your dad about that, by the way."

Gabriel took a step forward, then caught himself at the same time.

While there was *nothing* he wanted more than to join them, some abstract hesitation always held him back. Like he was looking at something from a story, and not his actual life. Like if he tried to get any closer, the image would suddenly vanish and he'd realize it was just a wistful dream.

He leaned in the doorframe instead, watching with a quiet smile.

"Stir the ingredients until smooth," Natasha murmured, reading from her phone. "Then gradually add the flour mixture." She paused. "Did we make a flour mixture?"

Jason dumped it inside the pot.

"Excellent."

She lifted onto her tiptoes for a better view, chanting quietly and making wide circles with a wooden spoon. There was something oddly rhythmic about it, like the cross between a conductor and some kind of culinary witch. But no matter what she tried, the end result remained the same.

Three...two...one...

"NO!"

There was a small explosion, then mother and son peered into the bowl together—tilting their heads at the same time. It wasn't the first time a culinary attempt had literally blown up in their faces. It wasn't even the first time that morning, though a new record was on track to be set.

After a few seconds, Natasha poked dispiritedly at what remained.

"I'm not going to lie...that looks *nothing* like the picture."

A hiss of steam rose into the air.

"I like it," Jason declared. "It looks like a volcano."

...it's not supposed to.

Natasha bit her lip, then glanced at the clock. "Alright, I'm calling it. Time of death?"

"O-seven hundred," Jason promptly replied.

She nodded gravely. "Jaqueline's should be open, I'll get something delivered." She wiped her hands and pointed down the hall. "Get dressed, then come back and we'll destroy the evidence."

The boy saluted and raced into the living room as she wandered distractedly to the windows and looked outside. It had been one of the hardest transitions since moving to London, learning not to panic when her fiancé didn't come back from a mission on time. His car was on the street, but he'd taken a cab to the airport. His phone went right to voicemail, but that wasn't cause for alarm.

That was when she saw his reflection in the glass.

"Gabriel!" She whirled around with a beaming smile, shoving the mixing bowl into the sink at the same time. "How long have you been—"

He crossed the room in a flash, silencing her with a kiss.

It never failed to amaze him, how much solace he took from that simple gesture. It didn't matter how many years they had been together, a part of him still thrilled like it was the first time.

"Sorry to be late," he murmured when they finally detached. "Something came up."

She leaned back on her heels, both hands on his cheeks. "You went to help Julian in Savannah?" She flashed a grin at his look of surprise. "Luke hacked into the GPS transponder. We were able to extrapolate flight records from there."

Gabriel blinked slowly, repeating each word back. "Luke hacked the GPS transponder—"

"We do each other favors," she interrupted with a shrug. "Every Christmas I help him de-frag the Abbey's mainframe." She paused uncertainly, staring up at him. "How did it go?"

The others had been on enough missions themselves they knew how to read the signs. A re-routed plane meant trouble, but Gabriel wouldn't be smiling if something had happened. His choice of wardrobe spoke to a lack of transportation. The pallor of his skin meant he wasn't seriously hurt.

Unfortunately, that still left plenty on the table.

And Natasha hadn't yet learned those signs herself.

"It went fine."

Gabriel kissed her on the forehead, steering her deliberately away from the catastrophe in the sink and towards the table. It was half-submerged in wedding paraphernalia and had become functionally unusable. In the penthouse up the street, Molly's table looked very much the same.

"Yeah?" she pressed lightly, still circled in his arms. "Any highlights?"

A series of images flashed before his eyes.

"I think Julian's a better shot than I gave him credit for."

She relaxed in spite of herself, notching her wrists behind his neck. "Is he anywhere near as good as me?"

Gabriel bowed his head with a smile, tangles of golden hair falling between them.

One might think that being a ballerina would have instilled some kind of precision when it came to marksmanship, but it had translated only into grace and not aim. The lovely girl couldn't hit a target if her life depended on it, but she was very good at keeping herself from falling down.

Carter had made her a 'field agent.' He'd done this with a secret smile. He'd also done it with fierce conditions from Gabriel—texted back and forth in the dead of night. She could go out into the field, anywhere she wanted, anywhere she was needed.

With a team of five veteran agents surrounding her at all times.

"No one's as good as you," he answered, kissing her squarely between the eyes. "After things settle down at the agency, I was hoping you could take me to the range. Give me a few pointers."

She flashed a grin, tracing a finger around his lips. "Oh yeah? You want a few pointers?"

"At *least* a few. Show me the proper way of doing things." He pulled her closer still, bending down to whisper in her ear. "Or we could always start now..."

A stampede of little footsteps thundered down the hall.

Incoming.

"Dad!"

Gabriel pulled back with a radiant smile, turning around as a tangle of messy blond hair flew across the kitchen and hurled itself into his arms. It had taken him a while to turn around. It had taken him a while to remember the title was addressed to him.

Now, he couldn't imagine a world without it.

"Good morning!" he exclaimed, spinning him in the air. He tried to get close enough for a kiss, but the boy kept turning his head. "You and your mom weren't cooking, were you?"

I smell treachery.

Jason pulled back, still avoiding his eyes. "Nope. We promised last time, *was* the last time."

Gabriel chuckled as Natasha flushed and glanced towards the sink.

"Good lad. You want me to drive you into school today?" He gave his fiancée a teasing wink. "We could always stop at Jaqueline's on the way. They're probably open..." He trailed off in shock, catching the boy's chin. "Hey...what happened?"

In a flash, Jason slipped out of his arms and landed lightly upon the tile—grabbing an apple from the counter before racing back down the hall.

"No need for a ride," he called over his shoulder. "Mom's already taking me."

A door slammed shut in the distance, then the couple turned back to each other.

"Don't freak out—"

"He has a freaking *black eye*, Natasha. What the hell happened?"

She lifted her hands, trying to calm things down. "I don't know. He won't tell me." She wrapped a preemptive hand around his sleeve. "And we're not going to casually interrogate him using our years of ghoulish espionage, or anything else that *isn't normal* and will *freak him the hell out*. He'll tell us when he's ready. *You* taught me that."

Yeah...in theory.

"Did he just..." He trailed off in frustration, hands balling into fists at his sides. "Did he just come home from school like that? Did one of the others say if anything happened?"

Jason kept things surprisingly close to the vest, considering he was all of seven years old, but Gabriel could usually pry any necessary information out of his cousins.

Especially when they were bribed with sweets.

"You don't want it to happen that way," Natasha reasoned calmly. She'd thrown a stapler out the bedroom window after seeing the bruise upon her son's face, but she'd had almost fourteen hours to compose herself since then. "You want *him* to tell you."

Again...in theory.

Gabriel stared a moment longer, then raked back his hair with a sigh.

Not for a single moment of his life, had he ever planned for becoming a parent. Having raised one infant in a place not dissimilar from the actual gates of hell, any dormant impulse or inclination had been ground straight out of him. But his life had never gone according to plan.

Jason was like springtime, like the sudden emergence of the sun.

Never could Gabriel have imagined the white-hot burst of emotion that would follow, never would he have imagined that anything could warm him so deeply, invoke such a profound change.

And *never* had he felt so completely out of his depth.

He blamed his training, he needed to blame something. Since he was three years old, he had been taught to fix problems, to carve his way past obstacles, to always—*always*—be in control.

But being a father wasn't like that.

It was model planes and too many race cars. It was reading the same story eighty times, then finding some inner patience to read it just *one* time more. It was why he studied his friends with their children in secret, and purchased every available resource to teach himself the basics. It was why he carried sunscreen and Dramamine in his glovebox, why he could sit down and tell you the plot of most cartoons, and found himself awake at four in the morning, doom-scrolling parenting blogs.

It was an endless learning curve. It would never be enough.

But if there was ever a kid to make you try...

"I want Jason to do a lot of things," he finally murmured.

Things had been difficult, the more time had been crowded out by the impending nuptials. It felt like the little family had just been hitting their stride before getting knocked back twenty paces.

Twice, he and Natasha had talked about postponing it. But given the absurd levels of guilt the child already carried, they didn't want to risk anything that might make him feel worse. They had been treading carefully instead—letting him set the agenda, letting him set the pace.

And now he's taking a beating on the playground.

"Can you just check his memory?"

Natasha lifted her eyebrows in surprise, hands on her hips.

"I thought we were never going to do that. We made a promise—"

"We also promised to keep him safe. And I can't very well do *that* if there are a bunch of little prats running around the schoolyard, hitting him in the face. I need names."

There weren't a great number of people in the world who would have stood their ground against Gabriel Alden. Unfortunately, all of them happened to live on the same block.

"Why?" Natasha shot back. "So you can strangle them?"

"...no."

She let out a patient breath, fighting the urge to smile. "I'm taking Jase to school today. You're going to get a few hours of sleep." She kissed him again, tracing the shadows under his eyes. "You've been doing too much lately. You need to rest."

He glanced down the hall impatiently. "I don't need to rest—"

She caught his face, turning it back towards her. "You *do*, Alden. I can promise that you do." She stretched onto her tiptoes, whispering with a little grin. "I plan on exhausting you later. You're going to need all your strength."

The anger ebbed as a reluctant smile played around his lips.

"Oh yeah?" he quipped, watching as she walked towards the door. A breezy dress hung loose on her shoulders, skimming above the knees. "And how exactly do you plan to exhaust me?"

She glanced over her shoulder with a bright smile. "We need to pick a table-setting for Molly. She's been jumping down my throat."

...That's just mean.

He nodded slowly, arms folded across his chest. He'd always had a good poker face, but it was hard not to smile when she looked at him like that. Most days, she won those little games.

"Oh, you thought I meant sex?" she asked innocently, before shaking her head. "I heard that doesn't really happen after we get married."

A teasing scowl flashed across his face.

"Don't even joke like that," he threatened. "I'll call the whole thing off."

"Love you, babe."

"I'm serious, Natasha. Not a single joke."

"Get some rest."

The door swung shut behind her, leaving him alone in the kitchen. He stood there for a moment, watching as Jason slipped outside and joined her at the car, before walking slowly down the hall to his bedroom—preparing to submerge himself in pillows and do exactly that.

He shouldn't have listened. He should never have closed his eyes.

Chapter 5

Gabriel sat alone on the park bench, watching the people ice-skating across the street.

It was just a day before Christmas, but he didn't know that. It was just a few days before a sobbing baby sister was about to burst into his life, but he didn't know that either. He was in a rare moment of calm amidst the perpetual storm. He was in a rare moment of unsupervised time.

Outside.

He pulled in a deep breath, fingers wrapping giddily around the bench.

His little face might have been calm, but inside, he was dancing. He could count on one hand the number of times he'd been allowed above ground since coming to live with the strange man below the church. The only reason it had been allowed that morning, was a sudden hiccup in travel arrangements for the *new arrival*, whatever that was supposed to mean.

Gabriel wasn't particularly concerned one way or another. He'd be forced to deal, whether he worried or not. For now, he was living in the moment. For now, he was watching them skate.

Look at her spin...

His bright eyes followed along as a graceful-looking woman detached herself from the others and started playfully showing off, dropping back her head as she twirled in a tight spin.

If it wasn't for a book that Jason had brought home one day, he wouldn't have even known what ice-skating was. His only experience with such a thing had been when Cromfield brought him on a 'talent-hunting' expedition in Nova Scotia and he'd fallen through a partially frozen lake.

It had taken the others a full minute to realize he was gone. It had taken the overworked healer another ten to revive him. To this day, he couldn't think about it without getting chills.

The noise had drawn him. His instinct had been concern, but none of the people appeared to be at any risk of falling. Quite the contrary, it looked like they were having the time of their lives.

His lips curved in a rare smile as he watched them flying around in circles.

They looked like a flock of birds, gliding across the ice. And the woman, he'd never seen anyone so beautiful. There was a scarf around her neck. He imagined it must be very soft.

"Are you going to the rink?"

He jumped in surprise as a child sat down beside him—a boy who couldn't be much older than he was himself. There were pink stains on his cheeks from the cold, and his nose wouldn't stop dripping. But he smiled easily enough. It took Gabriel a moment to recall he should smile in return.

He couldn't. He clutched the bench instead.

"I don't have any skates," he mumbled.

The boy nodded without really listening, eager to get on the ice himself.

"My dad's taking me," he continued proudly. "He's been in California for his job, but he's home now and he said we could skate for the *entire* afternoon." When this failed to make an impact, he glanced around the snowy park. "What about you? Where are your parents?"

Gabriel's pulse quickened and he didn't move a muscle. There were serious consequences for speaking to strangers, and there was a decent chance his keepers didn't know where he was.

"They, uh...I'm not..."

"Sam!"

Both boys turned in unison as a frazzled man hurried up the side-walk. There was a steaming paper cup in each hand, and a Bluetooth clipped beneath his hair. He tensed automatically at the sight of another person, then relaxed when he realized it was no more than a child.

"Hello there," he said cheerfully, coming to a stop. "Did you make a new friend?"

The boy took a cup from his hand, slurping down some cider. "Not really," he replied with a sideways glance, "he won't really speak to me."

Gabriel flushed with embarrassment, but the man took pity on him.

"That's all right," he said kindly, "some people are a little shy." His eyes made the same sweep around the empty park. "Where are your parents? Did you wander away from the rink?"

Unable to answer one question, Gabriel answered the other.

"I don't have any skates," he repeated softly.

A slight frown clouded the man's face, but the Bluetooth was already blinking.

"That's all right—plenty of other fun to be had." He glanced around again, hesitant to leave him alone. There were fast-moving cars, it was a busy street. "You have any plans for Christmas?"

Gabriel stared back with wide eyes. "...is it Christmas?"

The man stilled in surprise, feeling profoundly unsettled, then he took his son by the hand and escorted him quickly to the rink. As if the golden-haired boy on the bench was something to be avoided. As if he had something catching that might infect all the rest.

Gabriel stared after them a moment, then turned back to the rink.

The woman he'd been watching had fallen. The scarf was tangled around her neck. With a little sigh, he pushed to his feet and walked slowly across the street to the church.

Is it Christmas? Is that why there are so many lights in the trees?

GABRIEL SAT UP WITH a jolt—shivering slightly, like he could still feel the snow.

He took a second to steady himself, then glanced instinctively at the clock. It was barely coming on noon. He'd only managed to sleep for a few hours.

It's better than nothing.

He dressed quickly, grabbed a water bottle from the refrigerator, then swept out the front door to his car. His son was at school, and his girlfriend was at rehearsal. There was a whole slew of uninterrupted hours to fill until their return.

My fiancée, he corrected himself with a smile. *My fiancée is at rehearsal.*

The car sped off down the street, slipping into the familiar stream of traffic, as he drifted closer to the edges of the city and the rolling country that framed each side.

For a moment, he was tempted to do a quick drive past the school. There was a bakery across the street that had an outward-facing security camera. If the jackals that attacked his kid had done it anywhere on the eastern side of the building, chances were—

Your fiancée wouldn't be very happy about that.

He left the city behind. He drove to Guilder instead.

The Oratory was already in full-swing by the time he parked and pushed his way through the double doors. A group of shadow-benders were doing what could only be described as a creepy performance in the corner, but he was pleased to see that Julian was already back training as well.

It had taken a while for the psychic to find his stride after dismantling a human-trafficking ring in Budapest. Gabriel remembered driving him to the safe-house a few days after he returned, he'd never seen his friend so shaken. The whole way there, he'd kept hold of Gabriel's sleeve.

Julian had never noticed. Gabriel had never said a word.

"Nice outfit," he called, tossing his bag into the corner and joining him on the mats. "Did Angel make you change? That looks a little more her style."

At one point, the psychic had probably been wearing clothes, but he'd been drilling hard and before long, his shirt had been tossed in the corner. He glanced up in surprise, then flashed a grin.

"You want to talk about that?" he teased. "Me getting naked with your sister?"

Gabriel stopped cold. Men had been killed for less.

They had *actually* been killed for less.

"Let's spar."

Julian laughed a bit nervously, but waved him forward.

Present circumstances aside, Gabriel appreciated the gesture. Most people wouldn't accept such an offer. He'd been banned from sparring with PC agents before. It wasn't ever long before sparring turned to fighting. And it wasn't ever long before that fighting took a dangerous turn.

There was a reason people generally steered clear of he and his sister in the Oratory. They'd been bred in darker chambers, this was often reflected when they raised their hands.

"Hands up."

With no further preamble, the two men sank into a familiar pattern—testing each other's boundaries, defending their own, then hurling themselves forward in a dazzling series of attacks. It wasn't long before they took a simultaneous step back and tied back their hair. Just a few minutes after that, Julian jogged towards the bucket by the wall and grabbed himself an inhibitor.

Gabriel caught his breath, watching as he slipped it over his neck.

When he'd asked why Julian so often wore an inhibitor to spar with him—*him*, and not any of the others—the psychic had answered like it was the simplest thing in the world.

"I get better."

It was one of the nicest compliments he'd ever received.

"I'm surprised to see you here," Julian panted, dodging a strike to his face, before countering with one of his own. "I figured Natasha would be forcing you to sleep."

Gabriel spun around with a kick, catching him in the chest. "Are you the reason she keeps doing that? Are you the one whispering in her ears?"

He tried for another debilitating kick, but the psychic vaulted off the ground with an unlikely backflip, then swatted him playfully upside the head. They knocked fists, then continued.

"Of course not," Julian replied, taking a strategic step back. "It's obvious to anyone looking that you're spreading yourself a little thin. You'd think you were about to get married or something." He pivoted suddenly and lunged forward, only to get slapped on the nose. "You're a dick."

"You're an alarmist," Gabriel countered, falling into step once again. "What the hell does that mean—spreading myself a little thin? We're all spreading ourselves thin. I am *excelling*."

Julian snorted with laughter, but it faded quickly from his face.

As if on cue, the Oratory doors burst open and a group of men lumbered inside. Each of them was carrying a pair of chests too heavy for anyone without a specific set of ink. Each of them nodded curtly at the swarm of agents before pressing a secret lever and vanishing down the steps.

It had been weeks since Barnes had broken loose the prisoners being kept in the PC tunnels, but the repairs were yet to be complete. Part of the reason was an increased use of inhibitors. It was simply no longer feasible to reply upon supernatural protections that could be so easily taken down.

"It wasn't my idea."

Julian stared a moment longer, then threw him a glance. "What?"

"It wasn't my idea to come here," Gabriel repeated, waving him forward as the room slowly churned into motion once again. "Carter texted—wanted to know my availability."

Back and forth they flew across the practice mats as their shadows danced unnaturally up the walls. Julian was a hard opponent, one of the best. But if he was wearing an inhibitor, Gabriel could usually manage to beat him. His mind wandered as his body slipped into muscle memory, drifting back to those casual evasions and the violent bruise spreading across his son's face.

He wondered if he should ask Julian. He decided to table it for now.

"Oh shite—I almost forgot." He spun away from the action, taking a moment to remove his own shirt. "I need you to get a ministerial license."

The psychic glanced up in surprise before shaking his head. "No, I don't like pranks like that."

"It's not a prank," Gabriel explained, falling back into position. "Natasha and I want you to perform the ceremony and marry us."

Julian stepped forward, then froze just as fast. He couldn't remember the last time someone had managed to surprise him, let alone with something as important as that.

"You do? Wait a second." He raised a hand when Gabriel started again, pushing him gently back to create a little space. "You actually do? That's not a joke?"

Gabriel bounced in place, not understanding why they weren't fighting. "Of course I do. Why would it be a joke?"

The psychic stood there a moment, then bowed his head with a faint smile.

When he'd asked his brother-in-law why these tasks so often fell to him—*him*, and not any of the others—the assassin had answered like it was the simplest thing in the world.

"You're just better."

It was one of the nicest compliments he'd ever received.

"It's just...it's a real honor—"

Bloody hell.

Gabriel slipped a leg behind him and collapsed his knees—spinning him in the same instant so he was kneeling on the mats, caught in the world's most inescapable chokehold.

Julian let out a gasp, then tapped his wrist—staring up at him in surprise.

"You have to teach me that." He lifted slowly to his feet, rubbing his throat with a reluctant grin. "And yeah, I'll marry you. However many times you want."

A passing shifter snorted under his breath. "Devon's going to be so pissed..."

They flipped him off at the same time, then looked over in alarm as the door burst open again and a furious man stormed inside. He was followed by two apologetic case managers, both of whom were struggling to keep up with his long strides. But whatever supplications they were offering, he wasn't hearing any of it. When he rounded upon them, they cringed at the same time.

"Except I don't *know* where he is! Because I wasn't included on the *bloody* roster!"

Gabriel winced sympathetically, staring from afar.

Over the years, he'd grown quite fond of Rob Fletcher—a dark-haired shifter whose mighty eagle had saved them many times. He'd been partnered with another shifter, a wolf named Andy, since their graduation from Guilder. The two were bonded closer than brothers, and needless to say, he wasn't taking the PC's newfound policy regarding solo missions in stride.

He spotted them at the same time, throwing up his hands. "Can you believe this shite?!" he shouted across the mats. "Like we don't have problems enough, they send him to Oslo by himself! I need a freakin' tracker. *Julian*—get over here!"

The psychic flinched and removed the inhibitor from his neck. "I should probably—"

"Yeah, I'll see you later."

Gabriel watched as he made his way swiftly across the mats, nodding thoughtfully as Rob continued to rant, while casually escorting him to the tunnels. No sooner had they disappeared than the door opened again and Devon stepped into view. He stopped immediately upon entering, his sharp ears still hearing the distant echoes. He stared for a moment, then caught sight of Gabriel.

"What happened?"

Gabriel shook his head, feeling abruptly tired. "The boss sent Andy off without a partner. Rob's giving his case manager hell."

Devon threw him a sharp look, but said nothing.

They had each been feeling the increasing strain of the caseload in their own ways. A few weeks earlier, he'd been stranded without a radio in the Gobi Desert. Just the night before, his own partner had been sent to a gothic hotel, only to have been ambushed by the ghost of Christmas past.

"Carter's doing the best he can," he said softly. "You know he is."

Gabriel folded his arms, staring towards the tunnel. "Carter is insisting upon business as usual, despite the fact that half his agency just walked out the front door. Carter is jeopardizing everyone's safety just to prove a point."

"That's not—"

"It's true, Devon."

They lapsed back into silence, both staring at the same door.

There wasn't a single person left in the agency who wasn't thinking the same thing, but there wasn't a single person who could think of any better solution. Most missions weren't done for profit, they measured their caseloads in lives saved. If they were to scale that caseload down...?

"Why are you here, anyway?" Gabriel asked. "I thought you were on surveillance."

"Carter texted," Devon replied, heading towards the door, "wanted to know my availability."

Gabriel nodded absentmindedly, preparing to rotate to a different training course. Perhaps rings, or maybe spears. Then the words echoed back with a chill, and his head snapped up in alarm.

"Wait—*what*?!"

Chapter 6

There were certain doors one opened in the Oratory, and certain doors one did not. No matter which way you looked at it, Carter's office was at the top of that list.

But Gabriel didn't think twice before storming right in after Devon.

"Tell me this isn't happening," he demanded. "I need you to tell me that right now."

Devon glanced over his shoulder in surprise as Carter lifted slowly from his desk. In the weeks since the break-in, he seemed to have aged years. There were new wrinkles on his forehead that didn't used to be there, and his glasses had worn a thick groove into the bridge of his nose.

"Let's just calm down—" he began diplomatically.

"Why?" Devon interrupted, staring between the two. "What's going on?"

Gabriel gritted his teeth, glaring a thousand daggers across the desk. "Carter texted me the exact same thing. This is the time of our appointment."

It took the fox a second to catch up, then he turned to his father-in-law in dismay.

"You can't. You promised."

Gabriel opened his mouth to agree, then ended up shoving him instead. "What the hell is that supposed to mean? You exacted a *promise*? You should be so lucky, Wardell. They send us on a mission together, maybe you could learn a thing or two."

Devon shoved him back, but didn't rise to the bait. Instead, he gave his friend a pointed scowl and steered him back on point. "And is that what you want?" he hissed. "To be partnered on a mission together? And I don't believe for a second, you didn't exact a promise of your own."

Irritatingly perceptive.

Gabriel's eyes narrowed, but he conceded the point. "He's right," he declared, turning back to Carter as if the matter was settled. "It would never work between us. You need to find someone else."

"For *my* mission," Devon said territorially. "He'll need to find someone else for *my* mission, Alden. You're the one who's getting replaced here, not me."

Gabriel threw up his hands. "You don't even know what the mission is! It might really suck!"

Carter took off his glasses, rubbing at his eyes. "This is going beautifully..."

The men paused their bickering, turning to him at the same time. It was hard not to feel the slightest bit protective—the man was their mentor, and he'd been dealt a terrible hand. At the same time, they'd both exacted that promise for a reason. They'd done so within hours of meeting each other, all those years ago. Under absolutely *no* circumstance was such a pairing to be allowed.

"It would be too easy for me to kill him," Gabriel said bluntly. "You can't want that."

Devon whirled upon him once again. "You can't be serious. *That's* your reasoning—"

"I'm just telling the truth."

"We're in the freaking *office*, Gabriel. Not drinking in the backyard or fooling around with our friends. We're in the damn *meeting*." He threw out his arm in a furious gesture, waving violently at the chairs. "So how about you *grow the hell up*, and show some bloody respect—"

"It's Karl Weber."

The conversation paused as both men turned back to Carter.

It was a name that had become infamous in the PC hallways and tunnels. The name of a German pharmaceutical director who sold his drugs in neat boxes to the people of Western Europe, after testing them in dangerous and unregulated 'clinics' in Burundi instead. A few of the shifters had nicknamed him a modern Dr. Mengele. They'd never been able to reach him until now.

"I thought...I thought we couldn't touch him," Devon began uncertainly. "He operates with clean hands and you said the legal repercussions—"

"The man just put a four-year-old into a coma by prescribing him an unapproved blood pressure medication, then gave his parents the equivalent of fifty pounds to settle the bill. I could give a damn about the legal repercussions. We're taking the bastard down."

This was at least something upon which the men could agree. They nodded with the same muted satisfaction, arms folded across their chests. Yes, they would remove this lesion from the face of humanity. They would do it alone, of course. But that part could be settled in a moment.

"The man himself isn't the primary concern," Carter continued. "He may or may not be at the facility outside Gitega, our information is unclear. Your task is to recover the tech. His consumer algorithms, his case studies, the chemical formulas to his meds. He doesn't keep anything connected to a mainframe, otherwise Luke would have hacked him years ago. It's all stored on an air-gapped computer that he keeps under tight lock and key. *That* is your assignment. In three days, I want that computer sitting on my desk." He removed his glasses. "That being said, if you have a clean shot..."

Both men nodded in silence.

Over the last few years, they had performed many such tasks. Things that were left to the agent's discretion, decisions that were made in the moment and rarely second-guessed. Gabriel had made those calls with such casual regularity, that at one point, Carter had to take him aside. He didn't say a word in reprimand. He simply made him work in the PC mortician's office for a week.

He was slightly more hesitant to pull the trigger after that.

"I have you both flying out in a cargo plane tomorrow morning. Leaves from the east end of Heathrow, registration tag is *The Reconciliation*. I expect you both on board—o-five-hundred sharp. That's five a.m., in case you can't do the arithmetic."

The silent compliance faded, and the nodding came to an abrupt stop. Gabriel wasn't sure if *The Reconciliation* was a joke, but if it was, none of them were laughing. He was about to say something to that effect, but there was a chance Carter guessed it, because he was quick to speak first.

"There's also the fact that I'm not really asking."

Devon flushed and stared at his shoes while Gabriel discarded this without a thought. Of course the man was asking. They were the talent. They were required. When it came to negotiations, that gave him a bit of leverage. At the very least, there was room for a compromise.

"I'll infiltrate the facility myself," he said authoritatively, arms folded across his chest. "If you insist on me carting this one along, he can stay in the city and provide satellite support. We'll get him a radio this time," he added with a wicked smile. "You'll like that, won't you Dev?"

"This is something I can do myself," Devon said quietly, staring at his father-in-law like they were the only two people in the room. "Karl Weber—"

"Karl Weber is a two-man job."

"Then I'll take Julian—"

"Julian has a prior commitment with the Strauss family, and will be out of rotation until the following afternoon. The ship leaves in the morning. The window isn't any larger than that."

Both men pulled in a simultaneous breath, but could say nothing to dispute this.

The Strauss family had lost their eldest son the day Vivian Kerrigan tried to burn the city of London to the ground. Their younger daughter was leaving on her first mission and the psychic had vowed to keep watch. There wasn't a person in the agency who would dare to interfere.

"Okay, then I'll...I'll just take someone else."

"*I'll* take someone else," Gabriel interjected sharply. "Give me an hour to make some calls."

Devon let out a cold laugh. "Who are you going to call? Your sister's away on assignment and no one else is willing to play with you. Who are you possibly going to take?"

There was a beat of silence.

"Maybe I'll take your wife."

Devon threw up his hands, turning back to the desk.

"You see what I mean? I can't work with this—"

"You *can* and you *will*." Carter sank back into his chair with a sigh. "Do you have any idea how difficult it's been these last few years? Constantly shifting the pair of you to opposite sides of the schedule? Keeping you working on opposite sides of the globe? I don't understand why it's even necessary. You live on the same bloody cul-de-sac. You babysit each other's kids."

Devon muttered something about irreconcilable differences. Gabriel muttered something about having good taste. Carter gave them both the same uncompromising look.

"You go *jogging* together most mornings," he concluded dryly.

Devon took a step towards the desk, lowering his voice conspiratorially. "I only suggested the jogging to keep track of him—"

Carter held up a silencing hand. "*Enough.* This is my decision and I can assure you it's final. We're all making compromises these days, and Weber is too important to risk losing. The two of you will just have to work it out."

Devon shot him a bracing look. Gabriel remained defiantly aloof. "I'll bring him with me. I can't guarantee I'll keep him safe."

The fox turned to him slowly, unable to hear past the ringing in his ears. A hundred fiery responses rose to the tip of his tongue, but he swallowed them back—trying hard for patience.

"Is there anything else, sir?"

There's a good dog.

Carter shook his head slowly, eyes twinkling with a secret smile. "O-five hundred sharp, gentlemen. I have a feeling this will be one for the books..."

THE MEN PUSHED OUT of the office at the same time, realized with silent frustration they were heading the same way, then stormed in perfect silence up the hallway. They paused again outside the door, reaching simultaneously for the handle, before Gabriel shouldered his way through.

The Oratory had calmed down a bit since Rob's fiery entrance. At any rate, a piece of even juicier gossip was already trickling down. A passing case manager had whispered a few words to a conjurer, that were overheard by a pair of shifters, who felt the need to immediately alert the healers, as they would most assuredly need to be stocking up on pain medication and gauze.

Devon Wardell and Gabriel Alden had been paired on a mission.

The entire agency was already placing bets.

"So how about it?" Gabriel asked as they stepped onto the mats. "You want to take a page from your dad's book? Collapse a gothic tower, break every bone in your body. Call in sick."

Devon gave him a murderous look, then paced towards the punching bag. "I need to hit something..."

A past version of himself might have egged him on a little, but the Oratory and everything in it had suddenly lost all appeal. Instead, Gabriel swept briskly across the mats—pretending not to notice when the sea of whispering agents went suspiciously quiet as he walked by.

He was in his car just a minute later, screeching out of the parking lot and leaving the troublesome school behind.

It isn't fair.

His fingers drummed with manic energy on the wheel as he flew through the English countryside and headed back towards the city.

When the dust had finally settled from the sugar factory and Carter had offered him a job, he'd been dubious at best. The man had hounded him for the better part of two years before he finally signed the contract, and even then, he'd done so with a pair of strict conditions:

A clean slate. And a guaranteed lack of Devon.

For all his dark imaginings, he couldn't begin to fathom what a mission with such a man might be like. How would Devon have filled out his case reports? *Perfectly.* That's how.

He rolled to a stop with a faint smile.

Fair? When did I start expecting things to be fair?

He'd only just stepped inside, when there was a knock on the door. He tensed a moment, wondering if the fox had come to shoot him after all, then opened it a second later to find Julian.

"Hey," he said in surprise, "I figured you'd be a while."

The psychic slipped through the door. "Rob's taking the jet to Norway. Carter figured he should authorize it before the guy started collecting heads. Besides, you'll never guess what I heard in the locker room..."

Gabriel rolled his eyes, swinging it shut. "Lewd propositions and talentless tears?"

"I can't believe he's actually doing it." Julian paced into the kitchen, then turned around with a bemused smile. "Carter must really be scrambling. Makes me feel better about the shit-show in Georgia." He started to say more, then glanced up in surprise. "You guys moved the table."

Julian had a far better memory of places than most people, probably because he spent so much more time looking at them—whether he happened to technically be there or not.

"Yeah, it was submerged in wedding nonsense."

The usually immaculate house looked as though it had been struck by a festive bomb. Boxes of whiskey tumblers and gourmet chocolates had inexplicably multiplied to cover the entire mantle, while samples of tulle and fairy lights cascaded down the stairs. The table itself was half-covered in a wilted array of paper lanterns that had been briefly considered, before Lily sneezed cherry Kool-Aid and gave them such a gruesome appearance, the others had been forced to throw them away.

The men stared a moment, then shook their heads.

Molly's out of control.

"I was actually wondering if you could show me that trick you did in the Oratory," Julian continued suddenly, tearing his eyes from the room. "But I didn't know you were getting sent back out on another assignment. If you need to pack—"

"No, I've got some time. Come here."

Gabriel lifted a hand, beckoning him forward.

It was another thing he admired about his new brother—the man was unfailingly sincere. If something had truly impressed him, the psychic was able to put ego aside to learn it for himself.

The pair met in the middle of the floor.

"Inside?" Julian asked curiously, glancing around.

"Yeah, it's meant to be done in close corners." Gabriel put a hand on his shoulder, getting into position. "Internal security, elevators, that sort of thing."

To kidnap a sheik on the way to a cigar room. Not that I'm speaking from experience.

Julian nodded, standing perfectly still.

"Now this part you know..." Gabriel moved abruptly closer and looped a leg behind him, tilting the psychic off balance. "But it's the turn that does it."

In slow motion he took a step forward, forcing Julian to stagger back. At the same time, he tightened his grip on the psychic's shoulder and spun him around—half-collapsing his knees, while breaking the momentum of the fall, by lodging a firm arm beneath his chin.

Julian hit the ground with a stifled gasp.

"That's incredible," he panted. "They should teach us that."

Gabriel helped him up with a smile. "That's why your council hired me."

The psychic chuckled, tying back his dark hair. "I knew there had to be a reason. Can you show me again?"

The men went through the exercise several more times—discussing the different ways to counter, as they gradually picked up speed. Considering the potential damage of each repetition, they were actually having quite a bit of fun, despite the psychic's inexplicable efforts to keep things quiet.

When their legs knocked into a box of stemware, and Julian cast a nervous look outside.

"Just, be careful..."

At first, Gabriel thought he simply feared the unparalleled wrath of Molly. But his eyes weren't drifting towards the penthouse. They were drawn somewhere closer instead.

He pulled away suddenly, fighting back a smile.

"Does Devon know you're here?"

The psychic tensed in spite of himself. "I don't, uh...what do you mean?"

Classic.

"Does he know you're here?" Gabriel repeated slowly, savoring every hint of panic that washed across his friend's face. "Does he know you came over this afternoon?"

"You're being ridiculous," Julian answered tightly. "I come over here all the time."

Not for something like this.

Gabriel nodded innocently, reaching into his pocket. "Then you won't mind if I text him—"

The phone was slapped out of his hand.

The two men stood in silence as it clattered to the ground between them. Gabriel tilted his head with a little smile, while Julian flushed and kept his eyes firmly on the floor.

"It's just this once," he muttered. "He doesn't have to know."

Gabriel folded his arms, regarding him sternly. "That's what cheaters say, Julian."

"Could you just—"

There was a knock at the door.

Well, that's some truly impressive timing.

Julian flashed a startled look to the future, then his face went pale. For a split second, it looked like he was actually considering climbing out a window, but he didn't know if he'd be able to withstand his brother's perpetual teasing, and at any rate, the damage was already done.

The door pushed open as Devon rapped politely on the frame.

"Alden—you home?" he called tentatively. "The door was unlocked..." He trailed into silence, staring at the pair in surprise. "What are you doing here?"

Julian froze in a moment of sheer panic, then elbowed a porcelain vase off the table. "He broke one of Natasha's heirlooms—needed help destroying the evidence."

You saw it fall. That can't possibly work.

But considering the fox's keen observations skills, he could be exactly as distractible as the others. He glanced at the jagged fragments before rolling his eyes with a grin.

"Clumsy idiot."

Julian laughed nervously. "That's exactly what I said."

...unbelievable.

"I was actually hoping to talk with you," Devon continued suddenly, catching Gabriel's eyes and tilting his head towards the porch. "Do you have a second?"

"Sure. I'll meet you there."

The fox vanished and the men turned back to each other. Gabriel folded his arms slowly while Julian stared guiltily at the remains of the vase, determined not to meet his eyes.

After a few seconds, he knelt beside them.

"I'll just...clean this up."

Gabriel regarded him coldly, then headed to the porch.

Despite the awkwardness of their last encounter, Devon seemed determine to make things right. At the very least, he seemed determined to try. He even tried for a smile.

"Hey, sorry for just dropping—"

"What's up?"

There was an uncomfortable pause.

"So about this mission..." Devon raked back his hair, shifting nervously on the steps. "Do you want to get some dinner? Talk it out? There's this new curry place—"

"Can't tonight. I have plans."

He took a quick step back, walling up before Gabriel's very eyes. "Cool. Then I'll just...I'll just see you tomorrow."

Gabriel tightened his grip on the door. "Looking forward to it."

He watched as the fox backed swiftly off the porch, forgetting his own rules about using powers in public and crossing the park to his own house in a blur of unnatural speed. Their doors shut at the same time, and Gabriel turned around just as the white faded from the psychic's eyes.

"You have plans, huh? I don't see any plans."

Gabriel snapped his fingers, beckoning him forward. "Eyes on your own work, Decker." He placed a hand on his shoulder, preparing to run the exercise again, but he paused at the last moment. "This thing to-morrow...it's going to be bad?"

Julian flashed a prophetic grin. "I see nothing but great things ahead..."

Chapter 7

Gabriel got up the next morning, well before the sun.

He showered quickly, dressing in the same nondescript clothing as every other intelligence operative, then grabbed a pair of water bottles and ghosted back down the hall.

Natasha was submerged in the blankets, having gotten home late from a rehearsal the night before. She made some vague sound as he kissed her, but never opened her eyes. He stood above her a moment, softening with tender affection. How very *badly* he wanted to put that ring on her finger. Since returning from Cuba, it had yet to leave his pocket. It was there now, burning a hole.

Almost...not yet.

He kissed her again, then drifted to the room across the hall.

The bed was a tangle, but this time, not a person could be seen. Gabriel had to dig around a moment, before he glimpsed a wisp of blond hair. He rummaged a little further, unearthing his son with a tiny smile. At this point, he should be happy that Jason was sleeping inside the bed at all.

In the weeks immediately after the fire, he would open the door to find the boy pressed flat against the ground, hidden beneath the wooden frame. It was the same place he'd found him that fateful day—hands clamped over his mouth, half-choking on the smoke. Trying not to scream.

The smile faded as he remembered.

The first few times, he'd lifted him onto the mattress, only to return an hour or so later and find him right back on the ground. When that didn't work, he simply joined him—slipping a pillow beneath his head and lying down himself. Eventually, Jason found his way under the blankets, but Gabriel continued to sleep on the floor beside him, one arm stretching up to hold the boy's hand.

They'd never said a word about it. To that day, it had never been acknowledged. But Jason had clung onto him, even when he was sleeping. That hand would tighten if he ever tried to leave.

My son.

If it was possible, the word struck him even harder than *father*. The faintest whisper was strong enough to shake him to the core, yet he felt completely separated from it at the same time.

How could he be a father? How could he claim to have a son?

This beautiful child, this bright-eyed miracle who had somehow dimmed everything that came before...already belonged to someone else.

This was *Wyatt's* child. One of his oldest friends. A man who'd been recently murdered. A man who he was almost painfully jealous of at the same time.

He had the title. He had the claim.

And just because he wasn't there...

Gabriel stopped himself with a sigh, the same way he always did. With the gentlest of hands, he smoothed back Jason's hair and kissed his forehead—eyes lingering with concern on the bruise.

He should have asked Julian about it. When he got home, he'd do exactly that.

Sleep tight.

He swept out the door and locked it carefully behind him, taking in a deep breath of the crisp London air. Devon was already waiting by the curb, a bag slung over each arm, a pre-validated parking pass in his pocket, his phone set to keep him appraised of the weather in two time zones.

A virtual poster-boy of preparation.

Prick.

"Good morning," he greeted Gabriel with a tight smile, waving his hand at the car. "Since we'll be parking near the loading docks, I thought we could take yours. In case it gets stolen."

At that point, Gabriel didn't even have the heart to argue. He simply fired up the engine, waiting with increasing impatience as Devon loaded the bags into the trunk.

"Relax, Alden. This won't be so bad."

The fox had spent the previous evening getting talked down by his wife, and was making a valiant effort to shift his perspective on things. It helped a great deal that he was armed.

He slid onto the passenger seat, flashing another smile. "Just think of it as more continuing education."

Even Gabriel had to chuckle at that, easing them off the residential block and onto the busier streets. He might have had a few conditions before accepting Carter's offer, but as it turned out, the illustrious Privy Council had a few conditions of their own. Before being sanctioned as an official operative, he'd been required to undergo the same basic training course that each of the current roster had completed upon their graduation from Guilder.

There had been the usual classes, the usual evaluations. Target acquisition, coding and ciphers, interrogation 101. But there had been field work as well. He'd been required to shadow a 'real' agent on a 'real' mission before the higher-ups would grant him an assignment of his own.

Carter had apologized *profusely*. Carter had then sent him out with Molly.

Once he'd gotten past the debilitating blow to his ego, it was actually rather fun.

Despite being regarded by the entire agency as a bureaucratic joke, she'd decided to take her newfound role very seriously—stretching with him beforehand and lecturing about the singular importance of 'shaping young minds.' After graciously providing a notepad and pencil, she'd walked him through each step—bestowing little gems like, "Always check the locking mechanism on your guns, Gabriel," and "Righty-tighty, lefty-loosey," before finally pulling into a Starbucks parking lot.

"At this point, I generally like to hydrate," she'd said.

That was when he'd realized the actual mission wasn't until the following day. It had become clear around the time she pulled out a stack of wedding magazines and gestured for him to sit.

Party favors and mocha lattes. A 'real' Privy Council mission.

"Do you have supplies for that sort of thing?" Gabriel asked lightly, keeping his eyes on the road. When Devon threw him a questioning glance, he added, "Molly brought writing materials."

And stickers.

Devon shook his head with a wry smile. "I'm afraid not."

Gabriel snapped his fingers, steering them onto the freeway. "Another opportunity wasted."

"I guess so."

THE MEN DIDN'T SAY another word the entire way to the airstrip—staring through the window in stony silence, as Gabriel slid the car between two abandoned pylons and rolled to a stop.

They got out without speaking as well, boots crunching on the gravel and duffel bags slung over their arms. It certainly wasn't the first time two such men had been spotted walking towards the docks. If any of the people working at the glass company or the transportation services across the road had bothered paying attention, they might have thought it was highly suspect indeed, how pairs of grim-faced, identically-dressed adolescents kept vanishing into the cargo holds and never coming back. If they'd looked any closer, they might have even noticed the million dollar cars.

"There's a guy here I use sometimes," Devon murmured as they approached, "but I don't think he works any shifts on the weekends. We might have better luck just slipping into the—"

"Clancy!" Gabriel threw his arms open with a smile. "Comment ça va?"

The pair stopped in the middle of the pavement as a barrel-chested man lumbered from the ground controller's office and embraced Gabriel like a brother, lifting him right off his feet. Devon watched in silence a few steps away, hoping *very much* he wouldn't be greeted the same way.

"Gabriel, mon cher ami! Maintenant, je suis merveilleux! Et toi?"

"I'm doing all right," Gabriel answered with a grin, landing back on the pavement. "The practice is going steady. Madeleine and the twins send their best."

Devon flashed a strange look in his periphery.

"Listen, I actually need a quick favor..."

The man threw back his head with a guttural laugh, frightening a pair of disgruntled pigeons into the air. "Really? *You* need a favor? What a complete surprise."

Hilarious.

"That's hilarious," Gabriel said dryly, nodding his head towards the office. "Is that what you've been doing in there? Practicing your jokes? Whatever happened to Minecraft?"

"What is this favor? Since you're putting me in such an obliging mood?"

...good point.

Gabriel slowed the pace of the conversation with a smile. "That plane over there, *The Reconciliation*, it's heading to Burundi?" He waited patiently for the reluctant nod. "I was hoping it had room for two more passengers."

The man's eyes flashed across the tarmac, settling on the plane in question. "Not in the cabin, Gabriel—"

"The cargo hold is fine."

There was a moment of silence during which all three men considered what might happen if the favor was refused. After a few seconds, Clancy decided he didn't want to find out.

"I think she could hold a few more...but what about your friend, eh?" His eyes narrowed ever so slightly as they swept Devon up and down. "You know I don't like meeting new people—"

"I *do* know that," Gabriel interrupted with a smile, "but you don't have to worry about my friend, and I'll tell you why." He draped an arm around the fox's shoulder. "The man is a mute."

At that point, Devon decided to embrace his original misgivings after all.

"I am both mute and exceedingly wealthy," he interjected politely, reaching into the pocket of his jacket and removing an envelope of cash. "For your trouble, with our regards."

Gabriel blinked in surprise. Clancy blinked in surprise.

Then he reached over quickly and took the envelope.

"I thank you kindly, sir." He gestured to the tarmac with a broad smile. "They've already finished loading and the ramp is still down. Wheels up in about ten minutes."

Gabriel clapped him on the shoulder, hitching the bag higher on his arm. "Thanks, Clancy. I appreciate it."

"Have a safe flight."

The friends set off without a backwards glance, pacing in a deliberate line towards the aircraft with such confidence, it left no doubt to anyone watching that they were supposed to be there. When they were about halfway across, Gabriel flashed a sideways look.

"How much did you give him?"

"Five thousand pounds," Devon recited immediately, glancing over himself as they paced up the ramp of the plane. "How much do you usually give him?"

Gabriel tossed his bag into the hold. "I've never paid him before."

IT WAS ABOUT A TWELVE hour flight from London to Burundi. Twelve hours in an ice-cold, pitch-black cargo hold, with nothing but random phone apps to pass the time.

Truth be told, it wasn't that long for an intelligence agent.

But it felt a lot longer, when that agent's partner refused to speak.

I shouldn't have called him a mute.

Finally bored past the point of pride, Gabriel abandoned his perch upon the boxes and waded his way across the length of the plane to where the fox had settled on the opposite side. "Is this about dinner the other night?"

Devon was lying on his back, listening to music with his eyes closed. But he sat up when he felt the vibration of footsteps, pulling the headphones from his ears. "What?"

"The silent treatment. Is this because I didn't want to get curry?"

Devon blinked up at him, then pushed to his feet. "Are you *serious?*"

"I just thought—"

"That's so perfectly like you," the fox interrupted angrily. "What, you think I'm a child? I'm over here pouting because you didn't want to get dinner with me?"

Gabriel lifted his hands, holding back a smile. "It's my mistake."

"You know what I did last night instead? I had dinner with someone better."

Naturally.

"Glad to hear it."

"Glad to share."

It was quiet for a moment.

"What the hell do you have against curry?"

The men shared a dark look, then settled amongst the shipping containers once again, as the plane made a slow orbit across the sky. Devon tucked the earbuds into his hair and did his best to pretend he was the only one flying. Gabriel took a water bottle from his bag and slowly drained it empty. When he caught Devon watching, he took out the second and drained that one as well.

"Sorry, were you thirsty?"

Devon rolled his eyes and tried to angle himself in the opposite direction, but there was only so much a person could do while trapped in a cargo hold. No matter which way he turned, he could still feel the assassin's eyes. When it finally became too much, he ripped the earbuds from his hair.

"What?" he demanded.

Gabriel shook his head blankly.

"Why do you keep staring at me like that?"

There was a pause.

"You know," Gabriel began tentatively, spinning a blade between his hands, "I had to undergo *extensive* psychological training. Cromfield kidnapped a professor from Yale one summer for Angie and me. The guy took us through the courses, gave me an honorary doctorate himself."

God rest his soul.

Devon glared bracingly in the dark. "What's your point?"

Gabriel flashed an easy smile. "You're fun to watch."

They lapsed back into silence, one that was a little sharper than before.

Normally, Gabriel would have taken it easy, but the guy was *so bloody fun* to provoke. First, his fingers started twitching, then his shoe. Then he flashed a discreet glance across the plane, only to become immediately infuriated upon discovering his arch nemesis was staring at him once again.

"Stop that."

"What?"

"Stop doing that."

"I'm not doing anything."

"Stop profiling me."

Gabriel leaned back with a grin, arms resting on his knees. "Acute paranoia, that much is obvious. Definitely a few dissociative disorders as well. But with that level of defensive hostility, I'd guess there are some darker undercurrents at play. Perhaps some unresolved issues with your father?" he suggested innocently. "Or maybe you've finally come to accept the sad truth that I've been sleeping with your—"

"Do you actually want to do this?" Devon interrupted sharply. When Gabriel remained silent, he leaned forward himself. "You know, I had to undergo extensive psychological training as well. And as it turns out, Alden—you're rather simple."

Gabriel lifted his hands invitingly.

Go on, then.

"You know why you didn't get dinner with me last night? The same reason you accepted a three-man job in Cuba, but insisted you could do it alone. The same reason you rerouted a recovery plane to collect a stranded agent in Georgia, without even reading the case file."

A muscle twitched in Gabriel's jaw, though he maintained a careful smile. "And what might that reason be—"

"You're getting married in less than a week."

This is less fun than I'd hoped.

"You know what," Gabriel twisted uncomfortably amidst the boxes, suddenly feeling the claustrophobic space himself, "we can actually shelve this for later—"

"I didn't want to share a meal with you, Alden. But this was a last-minute assignment, and it could only have helped our chances to talk things through. But you don't want to do that. You'd rather go in reckless and unprepared, so that maybe, just *maybe*, something terrible might happen." Devon paused for breath, staring him right in the eyes. "And then you might save Natasha from making one of the biggest mistakes of her life."

The air went cold between them as both men went completely still.

In another life, Gabriel wouldn't have let the sentence finish. He would have taken the blade he'd been absentmindedly twirling and buried it with expert precision between the fox's sharp eyes. A part of him was still considering, but an odd paralysis had taken hold and he was unable to speak.

"Your words," Devon said softly. "Not mine."

You said them.

"You think you don't deserve this," he continued, his voice barely audible above the roar of the plane. "The best thing to ever happen to you—and you think you're not worthy. So you're careless, and reckless, and you self-sabotage every chance you get."

There was another weighted pause.

"Like this isn't *also* the best thing to ever happen to Natasha. And Jason. Like you're not holding together this spectacular little family with your own two hands."

Gabriel pulled in a breath, feeling almost dizzy.

His friend was coming at him from both sides—laying open the bitterest of fears, while countering with the most sacred of dreams. Sweet, to tame the sour. He tasted both the same.

Ex-friend. I suppose I'll have to kill him after this.

Or shake his hand.

"Me—I don't do that," Devon said plainly. "I wanted to be an agent, so I worked my arse off until I got hired. I wanted the girl, so I asked her to marry me, even while the world was burning to the ground. You start to do those things, Gabriel, but then you stop yourself—for reasons I can only assume have a lot to do with your childhood house of horrors and a deflated sense of self-worth."

There was a momentary pause.

"That part actually makes sense," he added thoughtfully. "You're a terrible person, one of the worst I've ever known. I'd probably have a deflated sense of self-worth as well."

In a bit of fortuitous timing, a sudden jolt sent them flying into the air. Another jolt was soon to follow, but at that point, they were already gripping onto the thick netting that secured the boxes. The plane let out a metallic screech as it hit the runway, then rolled to a gradual stop.

A crack of light pierced the darkness as the ramp began to roll down.

That's our cue.

In perfect unison, the men crept towards the sides of the exit, listening for the approach of footsteps, before dropping noiselessly onto the tarmac and ghosting away from the plane. It wasn't until they'd reached the road and lifted their hands for a taxi that Devon cast a sideways glance.

"So what about me?" he asked bluntly.

Gabriel locked eyes with a driver, waving him to the curb. "What *about* you?"

"Are you going to do my profile and even things out?" Devon asked, yanking open the passenger door. "Or do I have to keep an eye on that blade?"

I'd keep an eye on the blade.

"Your profile's a lot easier than mine," Gabriel answered, leaning towards the front and directing the driver towards the nearest the hotel. "I summed it up the first day we met."

The car shot forward into the dusky twilight.

"Care to enlighten me?"

Gabriel kept his eyes forward, still twirling the knife. "You're a dick."

THERE WERE ONLY A HANDFUL of hotels within range of the compound, but Gabriel and Devon were able to find a room in the first one they tried. A single room. This was standard procedure in case of ambush, one that had been cemented after several dangerously close calls. Even then, it was a procedure that both of them silently questioned before Devon reluctantly handed over his card.

They showered quickly, then split off to separate sides of the room—opening the window for good measure to make it feel like a bigger space. Without saying a word, Gabriel unzipped one of his bags and took out his weapons—going through each one of them with deliberate care.

It had been his nighttime routine for as long as he could remember.

Cromfield didn't schedule missions in advance, like the Knights or the council, and he probably wouldn't have given Gabriel any warning if he had. One learned to live in a state of readiness—able to pack up and leave at a moment's notice. Since he had no purpose beyond what the man had given him, along with no earthly possessions of any kind—this meant weapons.

Across the room, Devon was indulging in a nighttime ritual of his own.

That's a lot of pictures...

Gabriel couldn't make out any details, he could only see the muted flashes of light as they whipped across the fox's face. They'd been stored in his personal cell phone. A device that he'd taken with him on the plane. It was another potential risk, another deviation from protocol. But no matter how loudly Carter declared it was *business as usual*, no one in the agency was operating at peak performance those days. The photos were a comfort. They were all cutting each other a little slack.

And for one of the first times in his life, Gabriel was coming to understand that feeling.

There was a chance Devon was right. There was a chance he had been acting a bit more reckless as the wedding approached. But before that, he'd been cautious. *Abnormally* cautious.

His training might have allowed for more spontaneity, but he'd never had any trouble leaving everything behind at a moment's notice. He'd never had any trouble drifting without any kind of tether across the globe. Unlike the rest of his new friends, he'd never had anything worth coming back to. A part of him always assumed that both he and Angel would eventually be killed, and if he was being honest, there was a certain level of comfort in that—a certain level of security in knowing that whatever situation he faced would always be entirely beyond his control.

He could do nothing more than his job, *perfectly*. There was a grim sort of ease in that, one that enabled him to act without thinking, to stare with perfect ease down the barrel of a gun.

But all of that had changed. There were people waiting for him to return.

"You heard what I said, didn't you?" Devon broke the endless silence, shooting a bracing glance across the room. "About Jason and Natasha? Your adorable little family?"

Someone's having regrets.

Gabriel tilted his head in mock confusion. "What do you mean?"

Devon rolled his eyes. "I'm serious, Alden. You have this delightful way of listening to the first half of a conversation, and then shooting the person talking before you can remember the rest."

Sounds about right.

"No need to worry, we're all friends here." Gabriel flashed a dangerous smile, stretching out on one of the beds. "You heard what Carter said—we're jogging buddies."

Devon gave a hard laugh, settling on the other. "Right."

They flipped off the lights and lay there a while in the darkness—listening to the sounds of a city just coming to life. Things had never been particularly easy in the city of Gitega. They'd gotten even more difficult when a German tycoon had built himself a pharmaceutical compound just a few miles away. But the people had claim to a vibrant culture, and made their fun where they could.

Even from three stories up, they could hear the loud sounds of drunken laughter and the whirling spokes of rickshaws. The smells of fried plantains and nutmeg drifted into the air.

"Did you set an alarm?"

Gabriel let out a quiet sigh, staring at the ceiling. He hadn't anticipated the most harmonious of partnerships, but he was beginning to wish he'd left his friend in a cargo box on the plane.

"I set an alarm, Devon."

"Are you sure? Because these hotel clocks can be—"

"I set an alarm."

There was a pause.

"I'm going to set another one. Just in case."

Chapter 8

The problem with playing the time zones was that you were never really asleep, but you were never really awake either. The unnatural darkness of the cargo plane had already been enough to throw off the friends' circadian rhythm, and it didn't help that they kept waking up before the sun.

By the time Gabriel fully registered the alarm, Devon was already shuffling around on the other side of the room—brushing his teeth with one hand, and heating water for coffee with the other. There was a roll of athletic tape on the bed behind him, along with a pair of throwing-knives that Gabriel had never seen before. They locked eyes briefly, then he snapped on a lamp.

"We should get moving. Before the delivery trucks."

Gabriel nodded and reached for his bag, rummaging swiftly for clothes.

There were a few passing words, but the two men proceeded through their morning rituals in relative silence. The stakes were high, the tension was palpable, and there was something almost sacred about the preparation routine of a spy. Devon never said a word when Gabriel lined up each of his weapons according to size on the mattress, before concealing them in various places on his body. Gabriel pretended not to notice when the fox slipped in his earbuds and started looping the same quiet song—tapping the mirror three times, before heading towards the door.

"You ready?" he called, bouncing a little to stay loose.

Gabriel nodded again, and snapped the final weapon into place.

Here we go...

The stronghold they were infiltrating was only a few miles outside the city, but it was tricky in terms of terrain. Not only was the heat going to be a problem—considering they'd have to pose as air-condition mechanics or German pharmaceutical workers the second they arrived—but the land itself was also flat enough that they'd have difficulty concealing an approach. In the end, they decided to take a taxi halfway and do the last few miles on foot—taking great care to avoid all the lions, hyenas, and poisonous snakes they were absolutely positive were hidden at various points along the way.

Devon was still listening to music when they stepped onto the sidewalk, waiting for the taxi they'd flagged to weave its way to the curb. His head bobbed up and down, and his eyes were dilated with unnatural focus. He didn't realize Gabriel was watching until almost a full minute had passed.

"You don't have anything?" he asked curiously, taking one of the tiny speakers from his ears. "Nothing to help you relax?"

Gabriel shook his head. "He never allowed it."

At that point, there was no need to clarify who *he* was. There was only one man in Gabriel's life who'd ever reached such prominence as to have been implied. And it wasn't Gabriel himself.

If we're splitting hairs, that's probably a bit unhealthy...

"Jules got me into it," Devon continued absentmindedly, scrolling briefly through all their pre-game rituals and wishing the psychic was there instead. "Mental touchstones."

Gabriel actually laughed.

Yes, he'd heard the psychic use that phrase many times.

When a man spent so much time drifting out of his own reality, he needed something concrete to anchor himself, routines and muscle memory, invisible landmarks to guide him back.

"You guys have been working together a long time now," he answered, wishing Angel was there as well. "You have any good ones? Superstitions, I mean."

The taxi bumped into the curb, and Devon gave him a significant look. "At this point, we usually kiss for luck."

There was a beat.

"Get into the car, Devon."

IF THE CABBIE THOUGHT it was strange to be driving two identically-dressed Englishmen in the quiet hours before dawn, he never said word. The people of the city had learned to fear the dreaded compound in the wilderness, and avoided speaking about it whenever possible.

Their money was good. And they'd only asked to be taken halfway.

He left them on the side of the road with a quick word of thanks, then high-tailed it back to the city—never seeing the way they stared after him before wading slowly into the brush.

It was greener than Gabriel had imagined, matted with the kind of coarse vegetation he usually only saw from planes. Tangles of thorn-covered thickets and branchless trees gave way to sudden sweeps of grass—the kind that looked thick enough to stand on, rising up to his waist.

Perfect for a lion.

He cast Devon a sideways look, angling himself half a step behind.

"I've never been to this country," his friend remarked distractedly, making a constant sweep for predators himself. They both instinctively feared the things with teeth, but years of experience had taught both that it was the bugs you needed to watch out for. "The closest I've come is Rwanda."

Gabriel nodded in silence, his bright eyes scanning the grass. "I came here once, when I was about nine," he remembered the story, even as he told it. A great many of those excursions, he'd blocked out. "There was a man who could shift into a rhino."

Devon turned with a boyish grin. "Really?"

"Yeah." Gabriel grinned in return, without thinking. "I don't think Cromfield even wanted the power, he just wanted to see it for himself. He got the guy hyped up on drugs, then watched him tear around the savannah—ripped all these crazy grooves in the trees. When he finally circled back to us, he slipped into a strength tatù and caught him with one hand...tore half the guy's face off."

He'd never forget the image. It was a particularly terrible way for a man to die.

It was somehow even more terrible as a rhino.

Devon flashed him a look, but went silent, staring with a strange expression over the endless plain. They continued walking a while, but it didn't take a genius to guess his line of thought.

"You couldn't have beaten him," Gabriel said quietly.

Devon glanced over immediately.

He didn't question this. He was merely surprised.

"...not once?"

Gabriel shook his head.

"But surely you did—"

"Never."

The fox usually kept all such questions to himself—banned by his ferocious wife. But once the conversation got rolling, he had a hard time letting those curiosities go.

"How is that possible?" he finally asked, pulling Gabriel to a stop. "You could kill me in a second with your ink. A fight is full of such opportunities." He paused. "He didn't let you use it?"

Gabriel shook his head again.

No, he'd never been allowed to use that particular skillset. And yes, he'd considered doing it anyway many times. Many, *many* more times than his bright-eyed friend could ever imagine.

"But how—"

"Devon...I *love* talking about it."

The two men shared a glance, then his friend blushed and looked away.

"Sorry," he murmured, turning back to the road.

They continued walking the rest of the way in silence.

One was trying not to imagine all the dark machinations that had been brewing beneath the lovely church that had stood just a short drive away from his childhood house.

The other was praying for lions.

THE SUN HADN'T YET risen when the pair finally reached the facility, but that was by careful design. The best time for any infiltration was the hour directly before dawn—it was at the end of a guard shift, people were at their most tired. The light itself was changing, playing tricks on the eyes.

They stopped walking the moment they saw it, staring at the giant metal dome.

Way to embrace the natural aesthetic.

The place was a monolith, something that Gabriel could easily imagine being visible from space. There were no fences, or railing. No words scribbled on the side. It simply rose out of the earth in a seamless sheet of metal—arching about two hundred feet into the air before curving back down to the other side. There was a skylight on top, and a pair of doors that served as an entrance.

Aside from that, it was completely sealed.

"Not the easiest," Devon murmured, standing at his side. Every so often, a pair of security guards would circle the perimeter in lock-step. "How's your German?"

"Verpiss dich, Devon."

The fox flashed him a cold look. There was a chance he spoke German as well.

They folded their arms at the same time, staring in silence at the colossal dome.

Just because they hadn't reviewed the notes together, didn't mean they hadn't spent a good part of the previous evening poring over every piece of intelligence the good people at Guilder had managed to collect. The problem was, they hadn't been able to collect much.

It was a giant metal dome, one of them had summarized. Another had drawn them a picture.

"That's a clever design," Gabriel muttered, appreciating the simplicity in spite of himself.

Why spend an additional fortune on outer security, when you could simply insulate to such an absurd scale that the only point of vulnerability could be protected by a single pair of guards?

He stared a second longer, then shook his head. "You're going to think this is crazy, but sometimes the best way to get into these kinds of places, is by walking—"

"—right through the front door."

Yes, exactly.

Much as he hated to admit it, there were times that Devon surprised him. There were even times when he felt reluctantly glad to have the fox on his side.

"*Opening* the door is another matter..."

While the building may have appeared deceptively simplistic from the outside, the pair had absolutely no doubt that if even one of those guards were to break their rotation, or if that door was to be attempted by any unauthorized personnel, the entire compound would lock down in a flash.

It was a hard lesson they'd learned many times throughout the years. The easier something looked, the greater the likelihood it would need to be handled with extreme care.

That being said, nothing was truly impregnable. There was always a weak spot.

"What about up there?" Gabriel pointed, lifting his eyes to the sweltering peak. "There aren't grates in the surface area like you'd expect for ventilation. It must all come from the top."

Buildings were like people. They needed water and oxygen.

Nine times out of ten, *that* was the way inside.

Devon followed his gaze, tilting his head skyward. "Yeah, maybe..."

The height was one thing. The curve was another.

After a few seconds of silence, Gabriel threw him a sideways glance. The fox was still mulling it over, assessing the climb with a slight tilt of his head.

"Can you get up there?"

There was a pause.

"...I'm not sure."

Both modest and unexpectedly sincere. But his eyes lit up with the challenge.

"Hold this."

He whipped off his jacket and tossed it into Gabriel's face, pacing backwards with careful, drawn-out steps, as though he was counting. Gabriel caught the fabric instinctively, then dropped it to the ground, watching with vague curiosity as his friend prepared to attempt the impossible.

He paced back a few steps more, warming his fingers, but no sooner had he blurred past, than he came to a sudden stop. "It won't happen. The curve is too steep."

Gabriel nodded briskly, already moving onto a different strategy.

Since they had no access to air-support, which would undoubtedly force the compound into lockdown anyway, they might be able to try a subterranean approach. Such a thing was usually out of the question, especially given their limited resources. But with the combination of their ink—

"Can you bend it?" Devon asked suddenly.

He glanced up in surprise to see the fox still contemplating the dome.

"Bend it?" he repeated. It was a near impossible feat in its own right, especially from such a distance. But their problems were a bit more obvious than that. "You don't think someone inside will start to notice if the ceiling turns into convenient metal stairs?"

Devon probably would have cursed him, but his eyes were still trained on the top of the building, glowing with the same insatiable dynamism that got him recruited straight out of school.

"Not the whole thing," he murmured, "just little footholds." He lifted a finger, pointing to ascending spots. There, and there. There. "Can you do that?"

Gabriel appraised it a moment, then nodded.

Devon took a few steps back before coming to a sudden pause.

"Are you sure?" He waited until Gabriel met his gaze. "That's a long way to fall."

Gabriel's eyes flashed, but he kept his temper. "Do you second-guess Julian?"

A faint grin ghosted across Devon's face before he began the wind-up once again. "Don't say his name when we're apart. It's too painful."

This time, he started from further back, pacing to the start of the grass, before leaning carefully forward and touching the tips of his fingers to the ground. A look of extreme focus stilled his features, centering all extraneous movement upon this solitary, guiding thought.

His shoes dug into the ground. His lips fluttered in silence, whispering words his friend would never hear. But the second he flew past, Gabriel reached out suddenly and caught his arm.

It was a risky move. One didn't suddenly grab people with heightened abilities. It was a good way to get your arm ripped clean from your shoulder. It was an even better way to piss them off.

Sure enough, Devon stopped in the nick of time, glancing back with a flash of annoyance.

"What?"

"How will I know when to do it?" Gabriel asked quietly. "I won't be able to see you."

The dome had been designed to perfection, it wasn't like he could leave tiny divots in the roof. They needed to be there one moment, and gone the next—vanishing so fast that if it happened to get picked up by the cameras, anyone watching would see it as nothing more than a glitch.

Devon considered a moment, then he took the phone from his pocket and slipped the earbuds into Gabriel's hair. His lucky warm-up music was still playing. No words, but a strong beat.

"Count it out," he said softly, tapping the back of Gabriel's hand. "One, two, three, four."

He pointed at the same time, showing him where to make the holds.

Gabriel nodded swiftly, feeling abruptly nervous. "When do I start?"

Devon turned his eyes to the peak. "Start right now."

Just like that...he was gone.

Ironically enough, it was the kind of thing that was better when spontaneous. If Gabriel had any time to actually consider what was about to happen, he probably would have panicked at the last moment and insisted they try something else. As it stood, there wasn't time for anything but action.

With that soft music pulsing in his ears, he lifted a hand and marked the dome at the precise spots where his friend had indicated—levelling two fingers and pointing them like a gun.

One...two...three...four...

It was a lethal dance that needed to be orchestrated with the utmost precision. If he missed the mark, even by a few inches, Devon would likely fall to his death. And while the possibility of such a thing was usually enough to bring a smile to his face, he'd developed an irritating attachment.

He also didn't fancy having to explain what had happened to his wife.

"Come on," he breathed, squinting in the dusky light. "Where are you?"

There were a few terrifying seconds when he stared into the shadows, waiting to hear a burst of gunfire or the sound of scream. A few seconds after that, he was on the verge of reaching for his phone, half-expecting to see a text from Julian demanding to know what they'd done.

But a few seconds after that, there was movement near the top of the dome.

He took a step closer, squinting his eyes against the dull metallic glow, only to see the tiny silhouette of a person standing atop the colossus—both arms raised in victory towards the sky.

A flood of relief coursed through him, curving his lips with a grin. *He'll be impossible after this.*

Without a moment's pause, he sprinted towards the compound himself—pulling a weapon from his vest at the same time. He didn't anticipate any trouble with the guards, despite their parallel rotation. He timed the final approach and reached the base of the dome without anyone being the wiser.

The door swung open a second later, and Devon stepped out with a beaming smile.

"We are gods."

Gabriel grinned in spite of himself, pushing his way inside. "Easy there, Apollo. I'm sure it's been done before."

"By whom?" Devon demanded haughtily. "The mortals will sing of this day."

It wasn't until the door swung shut behind them that Gabriel understood why his friend was being so especially cavalier. He'd expected some degree of resistance—even in the off-hours, even in an off-site location, there was usually at least a handful of staff. But the room was just as inflated and disturbingly sparse as it had looked from a distance. Not a place to hide, not a person in sight.

"Where's my jacket?" He turned around to see Devon staring at him expectantly.

It took a second to click.

"You mean, that thing you threw at my face? I must have lost it."

There was a beat.

"My phone was in there."

Gabriel nodded, scanning the empty space. "That's not very safe, Devon. Not if you're serious about being a spy." There was another charged silence, then he tossed back the phone. The fox caught it with a scowl, doing a quick investigation when it didn't turn on.

"Did you take my SIM card?"

Gabriel bolted the door behind them with a smirk. "I'm going to wear it on a chain around my neck."

Like a prize.

Devon's eyes flashed with a hundred dangerous retaliations, but there wasn't time. Instead, he handed over a white lab coat he'd found in one of the lockers when he was securing the room.

He was already wearing one, having automatically given himself the superior rank.

"Now that makes you pretty much an intern," he continued seriously, flicking the acronym on the ID badge, "so I want you to speak with a certain degree of—"

"Hallo? Was machst du hier?"

The friends turned in unison to discover that the building was not so empty as it had initially appeared. A stern-looking man was pacing towards them, wearing the same overly-starched coat.

They lifted their hands in a simultaneous wave.

"Guten tag," Devon added cheerfully.

Gabriel shot him with a tranquilizer.

There was a gasp of surprise, followed by a quiet *thud*—both of which echoed with abnormal volume off the vaulting walls. Devon took a step closer, the smile fading from his face.

"Why did you...? Now we have to..." He threw up his hands in dismay, gesturing around the cavernous room. "Do you see anywhere to stash a *whole doctor*? You don't bloody *think*."

Gabriel rolled his eyes, hoisting the man off the ground. "I'm sorry, did you have a better solution?" He took half the weight and dropped the rest on the fox's shoulder. "Did you want to serenade him in German? Or maybe you could invent a little story to explain why we're both here."

Devon rolled his eyes and started trudging back to the lockers, dragging the body behind him. "I'm just saying, you're too quick with that thing. Remember when you got me at Christmas?"

Bucket list.

"As I kept telling you at the hospital—that was an accident."

There was a good chance the fox didn't believe him, quite possibly because he'd taken a picture at the same time, but they continued on without further mention. Along one side of the chamber was a pair of doors. One apparently led to the lockers, the other led to the stairs. They stuffed the doctor unceremoniously amongst the spare linens, then headed into the tunnels.

About halfway down, Devon flashed a sudden smile. "You think I'd be Apollo?"

IN A TRULY BIZARRE twist of irony, the subterranean levels of the compound were laid out in a similar fashion to the Privy Council itself. Granted, there were laboratories where there should have been offices.

And the locking mechanisms on *their* detention facilities were still intact.

Gabriel glanced in the cells as they passed by, relieved to find each one of them empty. They had been told that Weber operated primarily through the clinic in Gitega, but their presence would imply that at least some of the unsuspecting patients were taken back to the compound for further study.

And held very much against their will.

He paused outside the infirmary at the end of the hall, staring without expression at the pair of restraints affixed to the table. He was intimately with the feel of them.

Cromfield had a similar table himself.

"They never got a hit on the safe?" he asked tightly, rubbing at his wrists.

Devon shook his head, eyes fixed on the end of the hall. "Nothing was ordered, delivered, or installed for the last nine years." He paused a moment to listen, then eased them through the next set of doors. "There's a chance he constructed a vault of some kind, but even that would have left a trail..."

They stopped in perfect unison.

As it turned out, the boys at Guilder hadn't been able to trace the safe for a reason. The laptop wasn't in a safe. Nor was it in a vault. It was sitting on a table in the middle of the room.

Well, that's convenient.

"First the guards, and now this," Devon muttered. "Carter gave this order on a whim, he was pissed about that kid. We took a cargo plane. They couldn't have known we were coming."

Gabriel's eyes swept the room, latching onto the tiniest of details.

"Maybe that's the point," he replied, lingering on a forgotten sweater and plate of day-old pasta. "Maybe he didn't know we were coming. To keep this thing current, he needs to be updating it all the time. Maybe he left it out. Stranger things have happened."

Blame it on their gothic boarding school, but his friends were often under the impression that *bad guys* came with a rotating field of laser scopes and an evil cat. At the very core, most of them were simply businessmen. And in order to conduct business, there were times they needed to work.

"I guess," Devon said hesitantly, casting another look around. "But what about the guard rotation? Except for the two outside, we haven't seen anyone—"

Gabriel held up his wrist, tapping the watch. "One way or another, our window's closing. If we draw this out much longer, the night shift will finish and we'll get to meet all the extra security you could want. So unless you want to leave the laptop on the table, I'm taking it with us."

He waited a few seconds, then took a step forward.

"Hang on." Devon caught his arm, glancing warily at the empty walls. "Why do I feel like poison darts are going to shoot from the ceiling, or the floor's going to drop into a pool of sharks?"

"...because you watch too many movies?"

"Let's just take a second—"

"It's basic pressurized plating," Gabriel interrupted impatiently. "You can hear the buzz of it in the floor. But I won't be stepping on the floor. The laptop will be coming to me."

He lifted his hand and it soared across the room, fitting snugly into his palm.

"See?" he said condescendingly, blowing off the dust. "Everything's fine."

That was when the sirens went off.

Chapter 9

From that first piercing wail, Gabriel and Devon started to run.

It was hard to put into words, the white-hot spike of adrenaline after having tripped a security system. There was nothing people who worked in the shadows hated more than having their presence announced to the world. The taste of it worked into your mouth, the spasms crept into your hands. The belated fear of it was the reason that most spies eventually retired.

The ones that were lucky enough to retire. Many were simply shot.

"Pressurized plating, huh?"

Even while sprinting for his life, Devon managed to infuse such raw hatred into the words that Gabriel cast him a fleeting glance. He had taken the laptop—either as punishment, or by careful design. Maybe he intended to barter with it. Maybe he was planning to bash Gabriel over the head.

"Okay, so maybe it wasn't in the floorboards," Gabriel admitted, a red security light flashing across his face. "Maybe it was actually beneath the computer—"

"You *think*?!"

They leapt up the stairs and rounded the corner only to stagger immediately back as a spray of gunfire burst out across the room. Lots of gunfire. Lots more than would have been possible from just two people. It seemed their window had closed. The morning security team had arrived.

"That should make you feel better, Dev." Gabriel turned his face sharply as the fluorescent lights above them exploded in a sea of glass and sparks. "It's all the missing guards."

The laptop bashed him over the head after all.

It wasn't the worst odds that either of them had faced, not by a long shot. But as hard as the facility had been to enter, it was equally difficult to leave. The skylight was no longer an option, and those guards had clustered around the only door. Even worse, crackles of radios echoed across the chamber whenever the guns went quiet. This was but a single team. Another was already on the way.

"How many can you take down?" Devon threw him a quick look, pressed flat against the wall. "With your ink, I mean. How many?"

Gabriel bit the inside of his lip, trying to count them based on the firing pattern.

"Not enough," he murmured, shaking his head. When his tatù was used in such a directed manner, gripping onto a person's blood, it generally worked just one at a time. "I could try—"

"Don't," Devon interrupted swiftly, "the others would only shoot you." He flashed another murderous look, his eyes pulsing red in the dark. "That's something I want to do myself."

Gabriel opened his mouth to answer, then grabbed him by the shirt—yanking him back just as the ceiling collapsed directly above them. Pieces of debris rained down like shrapnel as they scrambled away from the wreckage, putting even more distance between themselves and the door.

"Did you have a better idea?" he demanded, emptying a clip of his own. "Our assignment was to get the laptop, Devon. One way or another, we were going to set off those alarms."

The fox opened his mouth to answer, then let out a painful shout as another explosion rocked the hallway—knocking them backwards and catching his sleeves on fire.

Shit!

Gabriel raced forward without a thought and tackled him to the ground—ripping off his jacket and using it to smother the flames. There was a muffled profanity as Devon pulled himself free and staggered to his feet, somehow managing to keep hold of the laptop the entire time.

"Are you all right—"

"Forget the door." Devon coughed violently, choking on the smoke. "We just need to get out of here. They know where we are and what we've taken. There's no reason to keep quiet."

Gabriel started nodding, then ended up shaking his head. "What does that mean?"

The fox leveled him with a bloodshot glare.

"We're in a metal building, Alden. Make another door."

I probably should have thought of that.

There was a sharp pain in Gabriel's stomach as he lifted both hands, flexing his fingers and aiming them both at the charred paneling in the hall. It wasn't a lack of metal—that was usually the problem. It was that the metal in question was absurdly, almost prohibitively thick.

Devon leaned against the wall beside him, aiming a gun at the entrance of the tunnel. "Any time, Gabriel."

He gritted his teeth and pressed both hands together, linking his fingers in a way he hadn't needed to do in a long time. The pain intensified, like an actual ripping in the walls of his stomach, and he felt each strand of metal as it peeled apart with an ear-splitting wail.

Inch by inch, he dug through. Layer by layer.

His heart was pounding behind his eyes. Trickles of sweat slipped like ribbons through his hair. For a split second, he didn't think he could do it. The image wavered, his tatù was throbbing, and he was convinced the strain was going to make him black out.

Then all at once...it happened.

A giant hole punched through the dome, and the pulsing shadows vanished in a burst of dewy light. The morning had come at last, gently erasing everything that had come before.

Gabriel let out a breath.

...ow.

There was a pause in the gunfire, a profound hesitation as people were sent to check the security feed and find out what ungodly force had just quaked the foundation of their impenetrable fortress. A bomb, perhaps? Some kind of targeted grenade? The air smelled different and they could have sworn the distant hallway had brightened with a trace of actual sunlight. But how was such a thing possible? The walls had been poured like a chalice, their targets were virtually underground.

"Are you okay?"

Devon's voice broke through the silence, catching him like a tether and dragging him back into focus. Both men had frozen the instant the light touched them, like some mythic creatures that had been turned to stone. One of them took a step forward, staring at the giant gap with a look of pure wonder, as the other bent at the waist—drawing in tight breaths and wishing he was at home.

"I didn't realize it was so thick," Devon breathed, running his hand along the seam. It was still warm, like the fading flush of newly poured metal. "Gabriel, I—" His head snapped up at the clamor of distant voices, getting closer all the while. "We need to run." He paused. "Can you run?"

Gabriel straightened up slowly, feeling like he'd aged fifty years. "I can run."

A single look at his face was enough to say otherwise, but there wasn't any time to linger and find out. No sooner had he finished answering, they took off once again—leaping through the gateway onto the packed earth below, and sprinting full-tilt towards the distant sky.

The world had come alive since they'd last seen it.

Flocks of black-tipped starlings dusted over the treetops, and the tall grasses rippled like waves in the balmy breeze. The door to the facility had been thrown open, and echoes of those deafening sirens blasted into the air. Their only stroke of luck was that people had been unable to climb through the wreckage of the ceiling. More people were still pouring *inside* to find them.

How long can that last?

"We should have rented a car." Devon panted, his boots pounding against the ground. He flashed a quick look, not at the army of men behind them, but at his bleary-eyed friend—the one who wasn't quite running in a straight line. "Alden—you still with me?"

Gabriel opened his mouth with a biting reply, then simply nodded.

His head was pounding, his body was aching, and he was likely seeing twice as many starlings as there actually were—but yes, he was still there. There wasn't any other choice.

"They're getting away!"

There was a screech of tires as a trio of Jeeps veered off the county road—taking advantage of the relatively flat terrain to chase down the intruders themselves. There was another burst of gunfire and both men ducked at the same time—scattering in separate directions as tiny explosions of dirt flew up at their heels. Devon threw himself behind a tangle of brambles and fired off two shots, hitting a driver and one of the gunmen. Gabriel went for a more direct approach and lifted the Jeeps themselves—grinding his teeth together, as he levitated one of them with each hand.

The tatù on his arm screamed in protest, but he was able to coax the ink to life—shaking them violently before crashing one into the other. He tried to do the same to the third, but the pain spiked with such overwhelming volatility, the world around him went suddenly dark.

"Gabriel!"

Devon appeared from nowhere, placing a steadying hand on his back.

He blinked open his eyes almost instantaneously, shocked to see that one of this knees had planted on the ground. He'd had mini-blackouts like that before, during some of his hardest training sessions with Cromfield, but he couldn't remember the last time it had happened.

"Sorry," he mumbled automatically, trying to gather himself. "I'm sorry."

Devon flashed him a quick look, helping him back to his feet.

They'd created a little distance after the collision, but the rest of the guards were coming after them on foot and the third Jeep was still heading their way. Even now, they could hear the crackle of radios, and the shouts of individual voices as they called to each other across the plain.

"You must take them alive!"

One voice had risen to such an unlikely pitch, that it trilled in a mindless panic above the rest. Sometimes it was in English, sometimes in German. Always at the same impossible decibel.

"Alive—do you hear me?! No gunfire, no grenades!"

Devon flashed a quick look over his shoulder, half-dragging his friend along. "Well, that's nice of him."

"You can get out of here faster without me." Gabriel panted, trying to pull his arm from his friend's grasp. "Get the laptop somewhere safe, then come back with a car. We can rendezvous—"

"Would you shut the hell up?" the fox snapped, tightening his grip as they raced across the plain. "I'm not leaving you behind. You think I'm just going to head back to the hotel while they take you prisoner? That's a pipe-dream, Gabriel. I would *not* be able to explain it to the others."

Gabriel flashed him a sudden look. "Who said anything about taking me prisoner?"

"They have my computer!"

The men froze at the same time.

My computer...?

In perfect unison, they looked around to see a face they'd studied in a hundred surveillance photos sticking out the window of the third van. Karl Weber had been driving back from his 'clinic' in the city and had arrived just as the alarms went off. And while he didn't have any idea how they'd been able to blast through his building, he was quite familiar with the laptop in Devon's hand.

Under no circumstances could he risk losing it.

Under no circumstances can we allow him to escape.

"Just leave it," Devon panted, his voice tight with regret. "We have the computer."

He was bleeding from a dozen different places and they were still being chased by half a battalion, but he was far more concerned with the man at his side. Only a few times had he seen an agent push themselves so hard. And each of those times had ended at a hospital.

But Gabriel had turned away from him, fixating on the man's face. "No, I don't think so."

He was seeing Weber clear as day, but for whatever reason, he couldn't stop picturing Jason at the same time. Those shining blue eyes, so bright and full of wonder. The dark smear of a bruise.

Without a hint of warning, he tugged himself free and changed directions—pacing with an almost eerie calm straight back the way they'd come. The image had steadied and the dizziness had inexplicably faded, every peripheral distraction falling away to leave room for this one man.

"Gabriel, don't—"

Devon leapt in front of him just as the Jeep picked up speed—catching the breaker bar with his bare hands. There was a creak of metal, followed by a silent curse. Then the driver opened fire.

"Stop!" Weber cried in a panic. "You could hit the computer!"

In perhaps the most surprising move yet, he bypassed his own security and leapt from the car—landing just as it fell free from Devon's hands. He lifted a gun of his own, prepared to do it himself from a closer range, but no sooner had he cocked the trigger, than it flew from his hand.

He turned in slow motion, staring at Gabriel in shock.

"How did you do that...?" he murmured in wonder, staring not at the assassin, but at his raised hands. "You have some kind of magnet?"

Gabriel stared back without expression. "You've been prescribing some nasty drugs, doctor." His eyes tightened at the edges as a stream of blood trickled down his face. "You've been prescribing them to some pretty small kids."

The man's face lightened in surprise as a battle waged on behind them. Devon was now singlehandedly fighting off the rest of the gunmen—using the Jeep's door as a shield.

"This is about the clinic?" he asked with an unlikely smile. "The clinic is the thing upsetting you? I thought you were after my formulas—"

"The formulas will be studied, then destroyed," Gabriel answered shortly, raising his hand once again. "Your security feed will be erased. But *you* will not be alive when that happens."

The man stared without moving, too spellbound to breathe.

"I would rather study you," he murmured, eyes gleaming in the morning light. "And I would not be so quick to kill me," he added as an afterthought, "not if you're after what's in those files. We have something in common, that computer and I. An incendiary device, with a bio-metric trigger."

Gabriel didn't blink. "You're bluffing."

The man shook his head. "I don't bluff."

No...I don't think you do.

At that moment, several things happened at once.

The Jeep whipped through the air, crushing the ribs of the final guard. The doctor leapt forward, only to feel a pain in his chest. The assassin closed his fist, stopping the man's heart.

And the computer exploded in Devon's hand.

IT WAS HARD TO REMEMBER exactly what happened next. Surely it would be extracted at some point, either by magic or some equally potent means. But for now, it came back in little fragments.

Gabriel had frozen a split second in shock, watching as the man crumbled lifelessly to the ground, before turning in time to see the bulk of the explosion. His friend was no longer standing where he'd left him, but had been engulfed in a cloud of smoke. A horrifying combination of blood, metal, and fabric haloed the ground around him—falling in a perfect ring of mayhem, as if to circle the person the fates had decided to snub. There was a muted cry, and a sharp impact.

Then Gabriel's limbs unlocked and he flew across the ground. "DEV!"

The fox had managed to release the laptop before it could completely destroy his hand, but it had mangled a fair portion, and a piece of the debris had struck him hard across the forehead. He blinked up in a daze, trying to reconcile what had happened, trying to see through the blood.

"What just—"

"Do you know where you are? Can you follow my finger?"

Gabriel knelt before him in a controlled panic, relieved beyond words that his friend was still breathing, let alone able to speak. He dragged him away from the wreckage before taking a grenade from the vest of a fallen mercenary and throwing it with expert precision amongst the rest.

It exploded somewhere in the distance as he turned back to Devon—stopping the incoming advance. He would answer for it later. He would answer for a lot of it later.

But first, he would take care of this.

"I don't understand what happened," the fox mumbled inarticulately, lifting a dazed hand to his head. He noticed his other a second later, putting it together at the same time. "The laptop..."

Gabriel bowed his head.

He thought the worst of it was over. But the worst was still coming. "We have to go back."

He glanced up in surprise as Devon shifted unsteadily on the ground, trying to raise himself up enough to get a better view of the terrain. "Why—for what?"

"For Weber," Devon answered, panting with the strain. "If we can't get the research, then we get the man. We don't need the computer anyway. Rae can pull it straight out of his head."

Oh shit...

"Devon—"

"I'm not going back to London without him," Devon interrupted fiercely, unable to make out anything through the smoke. "I don't care about the risk, alright? We need to find him—"

"Weber's dead," Gabriel interrupted quietly. "I stopped his heart."

He would never forget the look Devon gave him. Not for as long as he lived.

"HOW ARE YOU FEELING?"

The men had trekked across miles of African wilderness, running into a few of those scary predators after all, only to end up walking into the same clinic where Weber had done his work.

It was the mother of all ironies, but it couldn't be helped.

They weren't locals, after all. Not the nameless innocents who could be paid off beneath the table or disappeared without a trace. They were wealthy Englishmen—they had stamped visas and people waiting overseas. They also weren't sick. One of them had simply mauled his hand.

Devon had refused any drugs, endured a brutal examination, then bit down on the strap of his luggage while the on-call physician stitched up his hand. There was a bit of residual damage, but nothing that Rae couldn't heal once they got back. He'd taken a shower and slept a few hours, while Gabriel had gone into the city and picked up some food that neither of them was ever going to eat.

He was sitting in the window now, his feet dangling over the edge.

"How are you feeling?" Gabriel asked again. "Can I get you any drugs?"

Devon continued staring out over the city, speaking with a strange lack of affectation. "This has never happened to me before. I've never failed to complete a mission."

Gabriel stiffened involuntarily, lowering the bags of takeout to the bed.

He'd failed a mission precisely twice himself. Both times had been with Cromfield. Both times he had barely survived. He happened to know exactly how the fox was feeling.

And he happened to recognize that look on his face.

"You can't be angry with me for this," he said quietly, already bracing for the storm. "Karl Weber? The man killed *hundreds* of people. He would have killed more. Now he'll never do it again."

Devon turned around slowly. In a terrible way, he didn't seem surprised. "Is that what you're telling yourself?"

"You want to ask the people around here for their opinion?" Gabriel countered sharply, refusing to back down. "You want to ask the families of the victims—"

"Stop acting like a child!"

The fox might have recently had his hand reattached in a third-world clinic, but he sprang to his feet—turning away from the window, as his face flushed with rage.

"We can't make these things personal! We deal in lives saved, Alden! If we'd recovered the information from those files, we could have saved hundreds, maybe thousands down the road!"

"While innocent people suffered in the meantime!" Gabriel took a step closer, forgetting that parts of his friend were still bleeding and leveling him in a fierce gaze. "He was at the clinic *today*, Devon. He was giving unregulated medication to children *today*. He'll never do that again."

"And you don't think in one or two generations, someone's going to pick up *exactly* where he left off?" Devon countered with equal intensity. "You don't think it would have helped Rae or Ellie to study what was in those files? You don't think Alicia could have started working on a cure?"

He's right.

"You're wrong," Gabriel said flatly, pacing suddenly to the opposite side of the room. "It would be more stalling, more deprioritizing. More bureaucratic red tape. I'm not going to stand by and let it happen. I'm not going to watch innocents die while we play with numbers and statistics." He whirled around suddenly, meeting the fox's gaze. "Screw your numbers and screw your rules. It was my decision, and I'd make it again. These people are evil, Devon. They need to be *violently* uprooted. They need to be taken out of play."

Devon stared a long moment, then shook his head. "You sound just like him."

There was a pause.

"Barnes?"

"Cromfield."

A stunned silence fell over the room.

Not if Devon had been given a hundred years, could he have devised a way to inflict more damage. Not if he'd used his fists. Not if he'd used a gun.

"It's your decision, right?" he continued softly. "You're the one calling the shots? You're the one playing God? You are literally quoting lines from that playbook."

Gabriel shook his head, more shaken than he was letting on. "I just meant—"

"We don't do that," Devon interrupted.

Without another word, he turned back to the window—perching in the frame and letting his legs dangle over the side. He was lost in all but silhouette, but Gabriel could still see the judgement in his eyes. He took a step towards him, then let out the softest of sighs.

"Dev—"

"We don't do that."

He made it sound so simple.

Maybe it was.

Chapter 10

The men didn't speak to each other until they touched down at Heathrow. Even then, things were so stiff between them, Gabriel was surprised when Devon slid into the same cab. They continued to drive in such oppressive silence, it prompted their cabbie to turn on the radio.

What felt like a lifetime later, they rolled to a stop in front of Devon's house.

"Is Rae at home?" Gabriel asked quietly. "Can she heal your—"

The door slammed between them.

—hand.

The fox was gone before he could finish, sweeping up the front pathway and vanishing into the house. His lovely wife was indeed home, but she wouldn't be his first stop. He was heading for the punching bag in the basement, preparing to give his other hand a thrashing as well.

Gabriel blinked at the window, then stepped onto the curb.

"Tell me you don't live together," the driver joked nervously, lifting his hat to acknowledge the generous tip. "Because that man is going to kill you while you sleep."

The assassin flashed a tight smile. "It's not outside the realm of possibility."

The man laughed and sped off down the road while he cast a parting look at the Wardell's tidy cottage and made his way slowly across the park to his own house.

The cars were there, but the rooms were empty.

It's late, maybe they're asleep.

"Gabriel?"

He glanced up in surprise as a slender silhouette appeared in the door of his bedroom. She paused there a moment, assessing him in the shadows, then padded quietly across the floor.

"How did it go?" she asked softly, tucking back his hair. "What happened?"

He pulled in a breath, preparing to give her the standard answer, then his shoulders wilted and he bowed his head with a quiet sigh.

"I screwed up."

THAT NIGHT, GABRIEL and Natasha talked about everything. The rules of confidentiality were forgotten as he took her through the entire mission—hour by hour, step by step.

Whether she approved of his decision, she never said. She certainly didn't approve of his reckless methods, but that was a conversation for another day. For the time being, she simply lay beside him on the bed—crying when he couldn't, nodding in silent understanding, kissing away the self-loathing, and forgiving him when he couldn't forgive himself. Considering she never once slipped into her powers, it was one of the more cathartic discussions the two had ever shared. The kind that bolstered existing ties with additional strands of thread. When it was finally over, they slumped back against the pillows—both of them feeling utterly exhausted, each in their own way.

"You want some tea?" she asked after a long stretch of silence.

He glanced over in surprise, then chuckled at the look on her face.

"I won't subject you to anything else tonight."

Despite having made great strides in her continuing efforts towards becoming English, his future bride had made little progress in terms of coming to embrace the national drink. The American in her couldn't seem to brew the perfect cuppa.

"Are you sure?" she asked lightly. "Because I could put on the—"

There was a sudden clatter in the living room.

Gabriel froze unnaturally still, every muscle tensing at the same time. "...is Jason home?"

He was out of bed before she could finish nodding—spiriting down the hall and whipping around the corner, only to be greeted by the most unexpected of sights.

His son was not only home, but he'd also broken into the liquor cabinet.

"What are you doing?"

The boy whirled around with a gasp, having believed himself to be alone until the moment Gabriel decided to speak. His face paled as they locked eyes across the room, but he didn't let go of the bottle. Instead, he lifted it defiantly to his lips—wincing a little, as he took a giant gulp.

"What does it look like?" he answered, giving it a shake. "I'm making myself at home."

Gabriel regarded him in silence, no idea what to say in reply.

The boy had been through a trauma, there was no denying it. And given the circumstances, he'd done a remarkable job adjusting to his newfound life. But he'd only been living there for the last two years. There were still boundaries that needed to be tested, there were still lines to be drawn.

He took another painful gulp, eyes watering around the edges.

"Where were you today?"

Gabriel lifted his eyebrows, still hovering uncertainly in the frame. Both he and Natasha had vowed to be as honest with the child as possible, but there were still questions he knew never to ask.

He stood there a second longer, then took a cautious step inside.

"I was in Africa on a mission. It came up last minute," he added softly, looking the child up and down. "I'm sorry I didn't get to say goodbye."

Jason shrugged stiffly, fingers clenched around the glass. "You don't owe me anything. You're not my dad."

...there it is.

Gabriel froze perfectly still, feeling like he'd swallowed a blade.

It wasn't the first time he'd heard the phrase, the boy had said it several times before. Once at random in a grocery store, to correct a stranger's well-meaning assumption. And again when he was being carried away from the funeral parlor, a pair of tiny fists pounding against Gabriel's chest.

There had been a kind of progression to it. Not in sentiment so much as tone. In the beginning, it had been a warning—almost an accusation. Later, it was a reminder. Even later, an echo of grief. But this time was different. Gabriel couldn't quite figure it out.

"No, I'm not your dad," he answered softly. "But your dad meant a great deal to me, and you meant a great deal to him. So, I'm going to do the very best I can. Alright, Jason?"

The boy trembled where he stood, skinny legs sticking out from beneath an oversized shirt.

"It doesn't matter, anyway," he decided abruptly, swaying slightly on the floor. "I won't be here for much longer. This isn't my home, Gabriel. I'm not going to be your charity shop case."

At that point, Gabriel didn't know which stung worse, the words *charity shop case* or his own name. He knew the seven year old meant charity case, and he knew the kid was older than his seven years. He pulled in a silent breath, but gave no visible reaction. His eyes drifted to the bruise.

"Did the kids at school say that?"

Jason acted like he didn't hear him. With two shaking hands, he lifted the bottle and forced down another rebellious gulp—locking eyes with Gabriel the entire time. A look of sheer disgust rippled across his face, but he made himself keep going. The first few inches were already gone.

"I'm a man, now. I can take care of myself."

There was a pause, then Gabriel nodded slowly. "I understand."

"Don't try to stop me," the boy warned, wielding the bottle between them. "I'm leaving, do you hear? I'll be heading out as soon as you give me some money for the train."

I'm too tired for this.

Gabriel had woken up on one continent, only to find him falling asleep on another. His ears were still ringing with echoes of Saharan gunfire, he hadn't eaten in over twenty-four hours, and that searing pain in his stomach had yet to disappear. This was not something he was able to handle.

...but it needed handling all the same.

He stared a moment longer, then settled abruptly on the sofa.

"And where might that train be taking you?"

The child hesitated, sensing a trap. "Antarctica."

Don't smile.

Gabriel frowned instead, nodding thoughtfully.

He reached for his wallet and tossed it lightly on the coffee table, scooting over without seeming to think about it to make room beside him on the couch. At some point, a fire had been started earlier that same evening. The glowing remains were still crackling in the hearth.

"Antarctica, huh?"

The boy stared bracingly, then nodded.

"Well, in that case, there are a couple of things you're going to need..."

For the next hour, the two settled beside the fire and Gabriel talked him through the logistics—explaining the hazards of shifting weather patterns, which plants were safe to eat and which needed to be avoided, and the best ways to make a wilderness shelter in places with little cover and a strong wind. At one point, he paced into his study and returned with a topographical map he'd stolen from an antique shop in Brussels. Together, the two traced the ambitious route the boy had selected, starting in the Ronne ice-shelf and all the way down to the Amundsen Sea.

At that point, he would most likely start a colony and start preparing for what he could only assume was a very long winter. He'd spend his days befriending polar bears and catching fish.

They passed the bottle back and forth, talking until the child's eyelids grew heavy and he fell asleep upon the map. At that point, Gabriel picked him up and carried him back to his bedroom, laying him carefully across the mattress and tucking the blankets up to his chin.

"I'm not your dad," he whispered, smoothing back those sunlit tangles and pressing a gentle kiss between his eyes. "But I wish I was."

He stared a second longer, then closed the door carefully and wandered down the hall to his own room, surprised to see Natasha still lying awake in bed. She'd been eavesdropping until the guilt became unbearable. At that point, she decided to wait for him instead. For the last several weeks, they'd been having a rather delightful time 'practicing' for the night of their wedding, but despite the cozy glow of the lamps, she was wearing flannel pajamas, chilling out in the center of the bed.

He took off his shirt and curled up beside her, letting out a tired sigh.

"He was drinking the tequila? You let him drink alcohol?!"

He shook his head with a faint smile, turning off the lamp. "He was drinking the mix."

THE NEXT DAY CAME BRIGHT and early. Too early for Gabriel's tastes.

He rolled over with a groan, lifting a hand to protect his eyes from the stabs of light coming in from the window, only to end up faceplanting in a piece of paper on the other side of the bed.

He peeled it off slowly, blinking as he tried to read.

Taking Jase to get fitted for a tux. Remember to drop off those papers.

...should we just elope?

He chuckled to himself, crumpling it into a ball.

Ironically enough, he and Natasha had discussed the idea of elopement before. When he'd proposed, he'd been taken with the idea of a lavish party—all the flourishes and frills. Then he'd performed a quick internet search and discovered exactly how many flourishes and frills there were.

By the time he realized his mistake, he'd already asked Molly for assistance, and there was no putting *that* particular cat back in the bag. If ever the 'E-word' was uttered within ten blocks of her presence, there would be an ominous knocking and she would inexplicably appear at the door, eyes flashing with preemptive fury, like some kind of urban witch.

That's why Tasha wrote it down.

He tossed the paper into the trash, resisting the urge to swallow it, and wandered aimlessly down the hall—stretching out his battered arms with a yawn. Devon might have narrowly avoided the amputation of his fingers, but his wife could heal whatever injuries hadn't managed to kill him with the slightest touch of her hand. Most days, Gabriel would jog across the street and insist she heal him as well, but some wary instinct told him to avoid that particular house for a little while.

The adrenaline from the mission had worn off as he slept, and there was something about a quiet morning that brought all those pesky realities he'd been avoiding back into light.

He had failed a mission. He had actually failed.

Truth be told, a part of him couldn't get over the shock. He might not have been thrilled with his assigned partner, but there had never been a doubt in his mind as to whether he and Devon would succeed. They would argue, they would throw a few punches. But they would never *fail*.

His eyes drifted to the window, resting on the house across the street.

Go over and talk to him. You'll need to debrief, anyway—

He silenced the voice as quickly as it started, unable to imagine the cognitive dissonance that would be required for such a thing. If it wasn't the crushing blow to his ego, it was the basis of the argument itself. He understood the other side. He understood the necessity of thinking in broader terms and preparing for darker eventualities. But he couldn't reconcile the passivity in the moment.

"He was a monster," he murmured, staring at his own reflection. "He needed to die."

The voice switched tracks.

Finish those papers.

He let out a weary sigh, tying back his hair.

Finish those papers was a phrase he'd been looping for what felt like the better part of several lives. It was hard enough to get a legal marriage license in the country of England—a lesson he'd recently learned from his little sister—let alone to wade through the bureaucratic insanity that went along with adopting a child. It wasn't that he didn't have the necessary paperwork—he had all the papers, and all the certifications, in all the countries he could possibly require.

But they were all forgeries. And he needed to make this real.

"Alright," he murmured, "papers, papers..."

He brewed a strong pot of coffee, selected the first music on his phone with a pounding bass, and spread out what he'd already gathered on the living room floor. When there was too much to be contained in a single level, he added layers to the armchairs and couch. The previous iteration of his life had bred an instinctual need for organization, but Cromfield had also forbidden they ever throw anything away. One never knew when they might need to locate a diving certification in the Seychelles, or resuscitate an old alias licensed to perform veterinary procedures in Spain.

Almost eight years the man had been dead, but all those documents stayed in their neat, little boxes—stacked like a biographical library in the corner of his garage.

"Okay, citizenship papers," he muttered under his breath, scanning through the pile before discarding the document in his hand, "citizenship papers for *this* country—"

There was a knock at the door.

Thank the maker.

He lifted to his feet without thinking, his mind still on the task, then drifted down the hallway only to spot a familiar silhouette on the porch. His muscles tensed and he froze where he was standing—mouthing a choice profanity and shooting a furious look towards the sky.

"I can hear you standing there."

He lifted two fingers.

Can you hear me doing that?

"Come on, Gabriel. Open the door."

He stood there a second longer, wondering if he should take an extra moment to locate a gun, then he flipped up the lock and pulled it over with a look of false surprise. "Oh...hey. I didn't see you there."

Devon nodded with a hard smile. "Fascinating."

He tried to step inside, but the assassin didn't budge. The smile faded into a look of sheer exasperation as he stepped back instead, gesturing angrily to the porch.

"Right here?"

"Right here."

"*Fine,*" Devon snapped, reaching into his jacket to produce yet another document. "We need to fill out this case report, and since you're so keen to do it in public..."

He trailed off, eyes flickering over the assassin's shoulder. They lingered a moment, trying to make sense of the chaos, before brightening with a hint of a smile.

"...are you *filing*?"

Gabriel opened his mouth to deny it, but the fox was already inside—slipping mischievously past him at a speed that was most certainly not allowed. He slammed the door and hurried back to the living room, only to find him standing there with a peculiar expression, staring at the sprawl.

There was something unexpectedly vulnerable about it. Like walking into a roomful of strangers, then being asked to take off your clothes. He shifted uncomfortably, unsure how to move them past it, then Devon surprised him even further by doing the most unexpected thing of all.

"I'm sorry," he said softly, still staring at the papers.

Gabriel froze dead still behind him, wondering if he'd misheard. "...how do you mean?"

Devon's eyes softened as they swept over the room, lingering on all those broken fragments, all those certified people who didn't actually exist. His own files were much smaller, had been made by much different people. They didn't connect to his actual life, those lines had always been clear.

But those same rules didn't apply to his friend.

His infuriating, impressive, *endlessly* difficult friend.

The one who ripped holes in buildings, and threw cars like playthings, and put out fires at the risk of his own life. The one who flinched at things he shouldn't, and slept with the lights on, and stammered knee-jerk apologies when he didn't move mountains quickly enough.

The one who was trying. The one who'd put a terrible man in the ground.

"I'm sorry," he said again, turning around to face him.

Gabriel stared bracingly back, fighting the urge to frisk him. "...I'm sorry, too."

There was an awkward pause.

"Want to grab a beer?"

Gabriel found himself nodding, warming with a genuine smile. Then just as quickly, he grabbed his keys from the hook by the door, snatching a paper from the top of the pile. "Actually...do you mind if we run a quick errand?"

TEN MINUTES LATER, the pair was weaving through downtown in comfortable silence, arms draped lazily out the open windows as the summer breeze whipped playfully through their hair.

At several points, Gabriel considered saying something further about the mission. At several points, Devon considered taking the empty case report from his shirt. But the pair had encountered enough volatility over the last forty-eight hours, and were enjoying a momentary truce.

At least, in theory.

There was a whisper of sound, and Gabriel flashed a sideways look to see his friend's eyes dilated in concentration—lips fluttering as he chanted something under his breath.

"What's that?" Gabriel asked suspiciously, trying to pick out individual words. They were nonsensical and oddly parsed, almost like a song. "Some kind of mnemonic?"

The fox lifted a finger for silence, committing it to memory.

"...are those my aliases?"

In a flash, Gabriel turned on the radio—flipping it to a punishing volume as the entire car pulsed with the thunderous beat. Devon's hands flew to his ears as the handy rhyme was forgotten. "That's not funny, Wardell."

Devon flashed a grin. "It can never hurt to be prepared."

He grinned back in spite of himself, cutting across two lanes of traffic and swinging into the parking lot of a stately brick building they'd driven past without seeing a hundred times.

Devon peered up through the window, reading the sign. "The Registrar's Office?" he asked in surprise. "What are we doing here?'

"I told you," Gabriel answered, climbing out of the car. "An errand."

The two men walked across the parking lot, nodding politely at the security guard, only to find themselves in the middle of an overly air-conditioned lobby. Flocks of people hurried past in every direction, accosting the vending machines and queuing up behind the various windows. They were being helped by equally frazzled attendants, the kind who could have been identified even without their name badges by the repetitive stress injuries and glazed look to their eyes.

"Why are we here?" Devon asked again, stepping aside for an elderly woman.

"I got you a job," Gabriel said frankly. "It's time you found suitable employment."

Devon stopped in his tracks. "...please tell me you're joking."

The assassin had tried similar things before—having leased apartments and enrolled him at universities, anything to simply relocate his nemesis to another corner of the globe.

"I'm joking," Gabriel echoed for all that was worth. His eyes scanned quickly up and down the windows. "But it's a good fit. Having met you, I just assumed you were a notary public."

Before Devon could answer, he spotted the correct nameplate and swept briskly across the hall—cutting through the crowd, as the fox trailed silently behind him. A few of the attendants had successfully avoided the lines. A few of them took meetings by appointment only. The old woman manning the desk looked more ferocious than most, but she cracked a thin smile at their punctuality.

Devon read her title, then glanced over in surprise. "You *actually* wanted a notary," he remarked, watching as his friend took out a stack of papers and slid them across the counter. "What are you even notarizing?"

Gabriel pulled out his ID, sliding it towards her as well. "Jason's adoption papers."

Devon froze in his periphery, utterly stunned.

"Mr. Alden," the woman croaked in a dry voice, repeating the words she'd said a thousand times before, "do you solemnly swear, under penalty of perjury, that the evidence you've submitted in this matter is the truth, the whole truth, and nothing but the truth?"

"I do."

"And you've brought a witness?"

Gabriel nodded briskly, and pulled Devon forward.

She assessed him a moment, as if they might need to investigate his validity as well, before jabbing her finger at a blank line at the bottom of the page. "Sign here."

Devon cast him a quick look, then leaned forward and scribbled his name.

She pounded it with a stamp.

"Next."

THE DRIVE HOME WAS a completely different experience.

The windows were rolled, the music was gone, and the car was utterly silent. Oppressively silent. In a way that made Devon bounce his foot nervously and twist his fingers inside his sleeves.

At several points, he almost burst out with the question.

Why me? Why would you choose me for something like that?

But something about his friend's face made him hold back.

Gabriel didn't notice.

Those papers felt like a weight in his pocket, his stomach felt like it had been carved right out of his body, and the same tiny voice kept ringing in his ears.

You're not my dad.

"That was a pretty big moment," Devon said softly, eyeing his friend's remote expression as they finally rolled to a stop. "...how are you feeling about all that?"

Gabriel stared through the window as if he hadn't spoken.

He might have navigated them successfully home, but that's where the autopilot came to a stop. The doors were still locked, the seatbelts were still on, and the engine was still running.

After a few seconds of silence, Devon reached over and turned it off. "Are you okay?"

Gabriel sat there a second longer, then glanced towards him with a start. "Hmm?"

Devon hesitated, then gestured to the papers. "This is good, right? With Jason?"

Gabriel nodded quickly, slipping into a quiet panic.

This is good. This is the best. This is better than anything I've ever wanted.

He drew in a breath.

"No, it's not."

The world around him started spinning, and he dug his nails into his palms. It was an old trick he'd learned to keep things steady. Since he was a child, there had been a row of tiny scars.

"What am I doing?" he murmured, sliding his fingers over his face. "Why did you guys let me do this? Why did *you* let me do this?" he repeated, zeroing in on the fox. "You're supposed to be the one who stops me before I do something crazy. I can't just...I can't just take someone's kid."

The air was warm, but his body was chilled and trembling.

"I'm not his dad," he breathed. "He's right—I'm not his dad."

Devon's face went still. "...he said that?"

Gabriel nodded slowly. "The night of the accident, when I found him hiding under the bed..." He trailed off, shaking his head. "He was just so small. And he was *so* scared. I'd heard some of Julian's stories, growing up in a state home. I couldn't imagine Wyatt's kid..." He pulled in a quick breath, trying to steady himself. "But he's right, I have no business...taking something that isn't mine."

Just because I wanted him. Because I wanted him so bloody much.

He was vaguely aware he wasn't making any sense. He was vaguely aware he wasn't finishing a sentence. But Devon didn't seem to mind. He just sat there and listened, nodding on occasion.

"He told us that he wants this," he continued, a bit steadier. "Natasha and I have talked with him about it a thousand times. This is the decision we made. To become a family. This is...good."

Then why did it feel like he was choking on the word?

"Devon...I'm in over my head."

The car and everything in it went absolutely silent.

It could have lasted minutes, it could have lasted hours. He no longer felt as though he had any grasp on such things. But when Devon finally broke it, he did so with a smile.

"*That's* parenting."

Gabriel froze a second, then looked at him.

"You know," he continued quietly, "after Rae and I had a baby, Carter called us into his office, handed us a stack of papers like that. We were being sent out on a mission—both of us, at the same time. That had never happened before, not since Aria, and we had to make a contingency plan for if something would happen. We had to choose someone to be responsible for her while we were away." He hesitated a moment, drawing in a breath. "We decided on you."

Gabriel's mouth fell open in surprise. "Rae suggested—"

"*I* suggested you."

They stared in silence, holding each other's gaze.

"I remember looking at that paper, feeling the weight of it in my hands and thinking...I had no right to put a child in that situation. To leave them open to that kind of trauma and loss. Like a normal childhood isn't traumatic enough. Then the fact that we'd send her to stay with *you...?*"

He shuddered, and they laughed softly.

"But all I could think was...how do I best protect her? Who do I know that would throw themselves in front of a bullet? That would *always* be there for her, no matter the cost?" He flicked the papers with a little smile. "This is a good day."

The locks came up and he stepped out of the car a moment later, deciding to come back later with the case report, give his friend a chance to catch his breath.

The window rolled down a second later.

"You wouldn't have sent her to Julian?"

He paused with a smile, then turned back around. "Julian was out of town."

Gabriel chuckled under his breath, fiddling with the pages in his hand. It wasn't until a few seconds later that he realized the fox was still standing there, watching with an appraising eye.

"Do you know why you don't like me?" Devon asked abruptly.

This feels like a trap.

"Devon, I have a laminated list—"

"Because I chose this life, and you were forced into it. Just three years old, but everything was already decided—you were put on a path. So even now that Cromfield is gone, even though you tore that church to pieces, stone by stone, you don't think anything that came after can be real." He took a step closer, pointing up the lawn. "You bought that house. You fell in love with that girl. You rescued that little boy, and your friend would be damn proud of the way you're raising him."

Their eyes locked together.

"But you need to start trusting this, Gabriel. That's the only way it's going to work. You can't just live in the moment. You need to put down roots. You need to start making plans." He started walking away, then whirled around once again. "And if we're being perfectly honest, you might want to consider putting down those roots in America. Because I truly cannot *believe* you're living in the house across from mine."

In all the years they'd known each other, it was the closest Gabriel had ever come to liking him. He watched as he paced down the sidewalk, before unbuckling his seatbelt and heading to his own house. But instead of going inside, he walked around the side, wandering into the backyard.

It was expansive and neatly fenced, the kind of leisurely space that most residents of London would kill for. It was also completely undeveloped. Natasha had no interest in such things, and he'd really considered it. He and Angel used it to spar sometimes, but that was pretty much the extent.

He looked it over speculatively, glancing down to see a lone flower poking up by his feet.

"Want some friends?"

Chapter 11

A part of Gabriel melted when he discovered that baby plants were kept at a *nursery*. He'd seen those signs around London all his life, but never understood what they meant until that day.

He read a few lengthy internet articles, had an even lengthier discussion with an elderly Irish woman who had quite possibly sprung from the earth herself, then loaded his sports car to the brim and drove home with a smile—a potted hibiscus riding in his lap.

The garden itself was a different story.

A thousand bloody curses on the man who created this thing.

Gabriel panted with exhaustion, bracing on his hands and knees, while battling the dreadful contraption that was meant to be removing a strip of grass from the perimeter of the yard.

A sod-cutter it was called. There was a chance it was cursed.

"You will not defeat me," he growled, pulling on the handle until the edges began to splinter and break. "You will serve your bloody purpose, then I will strip you down to—"

It cracked up the middle, and he tumbled backwards.

"—parts."

He lay there a moment, trying to remember the man who'd dodged gunfire on the Burundi plains and juggled rescue vehicles for sport. When he failed to latch onto him, he cast a quick look around yard, judging the visibility through the cracks in the fence.

There was no one in the surrounding houses. The contraption had metal at the core.

It's just this once. And didn't Fiona tell me to find the magic in gardening?

Things went a lot smoother after that.

After the grass was removed and he'd poured the first layer of dirt, he was actually starting to have quite a bit of fun. It became quickly clear that his friends hadn't been exaggerating and he most definitely had a severe obsessive-compulsive disorder, but even that was working to his advantage.

He was meticulous, methodical. Perhaps even a bit meditative.

Over and over his hands dipped into the loose soil, coaxing in flowers and lightly scented herbs, helping them take root. It was simple work, straightforward. He appreciated that greatly.

The chilled beer nestled in the grass by his knees only helped.

I should have done this a long time ago. He tilted his head with a smile, easing a delicate sprig of wisteria into the earth. *I get why people are always going on about it. There's something really zen—*

"Alden, are you home?"

He jumped in his skin, spilling the beer into the grass.

And we're back.

"I'm out here," he called, never taking his eyes from the flowers.

There was a sound of light footsteps and the creak of a gate, before Devon stepped into the yard. He stopped abruptly short, like he couldn't quite reconcile what he was seeing.

"...what are you doing?"

Classic.

"I'm gardening," Gabriel replied.

There was a pause.

"How do you mean?"

"Think it through, Dev."

The man went blank.

"Like...to stash things?" he finally ventured. "Hibiscus is for handguns, poppies are for powdered carcinogens—that kind of thing? Wouldn't it be easier with open ground?"

"It isn't to stash things," Gabriel said patiently. "I want to have a garden." He glanced over his shoulder to see his friend standing at a loss behind him, his head cocked to the side in a way that was strangely reminiscent of the fox etched onto his arm. "How did you know these were hibiscus?"

Devon stared a second longer, then shrugged. "My mom had a garden, she taught me." He glanced around the yard, still feeling a bit off-balanced by the whole affair. "Rae's always been more interested in *getting* flowers..."

Gabriel nodded, then glanced back with a smile. "Your mom?"

Devon bristled defensively. "Some of us have parents, orphan."

"Yeah, alright. Help me with this."

Together, the two men walked back to the porch and heaved the remaining bags of dirt over to the fence—ripping them open and scattering the contents along the grass. It was tough work, the kind that made you feel the sun upon your shoulders. But there was an undeniable satisfaction to it.

After they emptied the final one, even Devon was looking rather pleased.

And completely bewildered.

"Why are you doing this?"

Gabriel dusted his hands, flashing a crooked grin. "I'm putting down roots."

There was a beat of silence.

"You're so freakin' literal." He laughed despite himself. Wiping he hands on his pants, he added, "I need to go over this case report with you."

"I'm busy."

Devon paused another moment, considering. "You're having a mental break," he decided. "That can wait—"

"I'm *busy*," Gabriel repeated, burying his hands up to the wrists. He even liked the feel of the soil—cool, while everything else was so hot. "I'm tending to my flock."

Alright, so it's a BIT of a God-complex.

"Can't you take ten minutes—"

He threw a sharp look over his shoulder, repeating what the woman at the nursery had told him. "*Devon*...they're coming into bloom."

This brought a stunned end to the conversation. For the life of him, Devon could think of nothing to say. There was an urgency he couldn't question, yet didn't remotely understand.

After a long silence, he tried for a compromise.

"How about I sit here and read it to you?"

"Knock yourself out."

Use the sod-cutter.

Devon proceeded to settle himself at the patio table, flipping open the first page and pulling out a pen. It was a standard form, one he could easily have done himself. But given that they had been sent on the mission together, they were both required to partake.

"Alright first question," he murmured, reading aloud, "how could your communication have been improved—" He caught himself quickly and started scribbling. "Well, I can answer that..."

Gabriel tuned him out with relative ease, working his way slowly down the row. It hadn't taken long to catch the rhythm of things, and he was already about a quarter of the way through planting the things he'd bought. He was so consumed in the task, so thoroughly immersed, it took a second to realize that Devon had stopped the questionnaire and was watching him instead.

Not watching—*critiquing.*

Without realizing what he was doing, he pushed slowly to his feet—biting the inside of his lip, as he squinted into the sun. "You're putting the orange ones over there?"

"They do better in direct sunlight," Gabriel panted, wiping his brow. "At least, that's what it says on the carton."

Devon cast a dubious look at the English sky. "Well, if that's the case, why don't you—"

"You want to do it yourself?"

The fox paused a moment, wondering if his friend was merely being sarcastic, or if it was a genuine offer. In the end, he decided to embrace the invitation either way. "Yeah, alright."

Without a second thought, he tossed the case report onto the table and ventured into the garden himself—confiscating the orange blossoms and relocating them with a boyish grin.

Another beer was produced. Then another after that. The boys were actually having a fine time, when the gate swung open again and a stunning redhead—auburn-headed female—stepped into the yard.

"...what the *bloody hell* is going on?"

They glanced up with matching smiles.

"We're gardening."

Rae took a second to process, then decided she didn't approve.

"Oh, I see. So while I'm trapped in that glorious penthouse, slaving away over table settings and French cheese, you guys are literally playing around in the dirt—"

"We're planting different options for the boutonnieres," Gabriel interrupted with a sudden burst of inspiration. "We want to see how they look in direct sunlight before making a choice."

There was a terrifying moment of silence.

"Well, that's...a *brilliant* idea." Her face warmed with a radiant smile.

"I'm proud of you, Gabriel. You're really taking this seriously. And you—helping him." She beamed at Devon before taking off her purse and slinging it onto the table. "Well, I had a meeting scheduled at the Swiss embassy, but this is much more important. How can I help?"

IT WAS ONE OF THE BEST days that Gabriel could remember.

One by one, all of his friends trickled into the yard.

They each started the same way—enraged that no one was answering their phones, deeply concerned as to why they'd decided to garden, then gradually coming around to the idea themselves.

Albeit, each with their own unique style.

Molly simply picked her favorite and spread it gleefully across the yard, while Luke provided a cheerful balance, one of the few who actually managed to help. Julian handled the contemplative silences better than most—sinking into the meditative aspect with a smile that made the others wonder if he'd start a garden himself, while Angel was better suited to attacking the weeds.

Rae conjured a set of windchimes and stared at them expectantly.

A second later, she also conjured some wind.

At one point, Devon attempted to co-opt the experience.

"Alright, guys, we're putting the perennials in the southeast corner, and anything that belongs to the nightshade family, we should probably just throw away—"

Gabriel turned to him slowly, and he raised his hands.

"I mean...I'm just guessing. It's your garden."

And so it continued, as the sun made a slow arc across the sky.

They were all generally rubbish. His sister, in particular, was a bit of a nasty touch. But by the end of the day, the garden was planted and they found themselves sitting on the lawn in contented silence, staring towards the heavens, as the sun gave way to a sky full of stars.

The gate swung open once again.

"Let me guess...you all watched *FernGully*."

The friends turned in unison as two more people stepped into the yard. Jason made a beeline for the windchimes, blowing on them with all his might, while Natasha swept across the grass towards Gabriel—a formal garment bag slung over her arm.

"I see you've been busy," she murmured, eyes twinkling with a smile.

Molly sprang excitedly to her feet, reaching in between as they tried to kiss.

"Oh—this is perfect!" she squealed, unzipping the corner and peeking inside. "It's going to look so great next to the suit I reserved for Angel."

"The suit?" Gabriel asked in confusion. "She's not wearing a dress?"

Molly glanced between them, all her momentum stalling on a dime. "Oh, I just...I just assumed Angel would be the best man."

Angel glanced over with a shrug, completely unconcerned either way.

"Actually...I've already got a best man," Gabriel said leadingly, looking over her shoulder and locking eyes with his son. "That's if he says yes."

The others turned in the same direction, waiting with a collective smile.

But they would be waiting a long time.

Jason froze under the sudden spotlight, tensing with the same expression he got whenever he walked past the wedding paraphilia that was slowly taking over the house. A look of silent panic swept over him before he shook his head quickly, backing towards the door.

"I...I don't think that's a good idea," he stammered. "It should probably be a grown-up."

Gabriel went still for a second, then nodded quickly. "Yeah, of course. Whatever you want."

The child nodded hastily, then vanished into the house—leaving an awkward silence in his wake. The others shared a quick glance, as Natasha took his hand, giving it a little squeeze.

"Some people need more time than others," she murmured.

He nodded again, pretending not to hear Molly whisper behind his back.

"I'll put that suit on hold...just in case."

THE SUNLIT DAY ENDED with an unexpected chill, but there was still plenty of memories to be made. Natasha took one look at the adoption papers, then burst into tears—holding them to her chest and sinking right down in the middle of the stairs. Gabriel carried her to their room, where they proceeded to read through each word together. Then they did it again. And again after that.

They finished the evening with a shared bubble-bath, which turned into a bit more wedding practice, before they curled up together under the covers—drifting off into a peaceful sleep.

The door creaked open a few hours later, piercing the room with a crack of light.

"...dad?"

Gabriel bolted upright in a flash, one hand securing a sleeping Natasha, as the other reached automatically for his gun. He caught himself a second later, blinking at the boy in the frame.

"Jase? What's wrong?"

There was a pause.

"I had a bad dream."

Five minutes later, the pair had relocated to the kitchen. Jason was perched atop the counter, feeling a bit embarrassed, while Gabriel rummaged in the cupboards—pouring him a glass of water.

"Here you go," he murmured, "little sips."

Jason took it with both hands, staring over the rim. "You have a lot of scars," he said tentatively. "How did you get them?"

Gabriel froze in surprise, thrown completely off guard.

He sometimes forgot how new they were to each other. Just the other night, he'd brought home Italian takeout for dinner, not knowing the child was allergic to mushrooms.

"I got them all sorts of ways," he answered, slipping on a shirt. "You want to tell me about the dream?" Jason hesitated a moment, then shook his head. "That's okay, we can just—"

"I'm sorry about earlier."

A ringing silence fell between them.

"When you asked me..." He trailed off, looking completely overwhelmed. "I didn't know how to..." His eyes dropped miserably to the floor. "I didn't want to hurt your feelings."

Please—just let me hold you.

"You didn't hurt my feelings," Gabriel said softly. When the boy wouldn't look at him, he crossed the room, coaxing up his eyes. "Hey, you didn't hurt my feelings." He paused a moment, debating whether to continue. "You know I finalized the adoption papers today?"

Jason nodded silently, staring at the floor. "Yeah, Mom told me."

There was another pause.

"Is that...is that something you'd like to talk about?" Gabriel regarded him intently, unable to pull in a breath. "Jase, if this is all moving too fast, we can slow it down—"

"It's not moving too fast."

Another silence. Another tailspin.

That's parenting.

Maybe Devon meant it as a joke.

"Alright—good." He raked back his hair, intentionally smoothing his fingers before those nails could dig into his palms. "Then how about we—"

"Could you maybe sleep in my room tonight?" Jason interjected suddenly. Those blue eyes ventured upwards, resting uncertainly on his father's face. "In case the dream comes back?"

Gabriel stared at him a moment, then his face warmed with a smile. "Yeah, I could do that."

TEN MINUTES LATER, the boy was fast asleep.

Gabriel had walked him silently down the hall, preparing to stretch out on the floorboards like he was used to, only to have a little hand flash out and catch his sleeve. They lay down on the mattress instead—one settling across the length of the wooden frame, while the other tucked into his arm. *Onto* his arm, there was no longer any moving it. All the strange and impossible contortions Gabriel had found himself in throughout the years—cramped in a sewage tunnel, hiding in a ventilation shaft, wedging his body into the smuggler's compartment of a stolen truck—he had never been so still. He lay there for hours without moving, without breathing, without shifting his eyes in the slightest direction, lest the spell be broken and the child would somehow wake up.

It was one of the best nights of his life.

Chapter 12

Gabriel sensed Rae coming before he actually saw her, followed her shadow as it moved across the wall. By the time she broke inside and cracked open the bedroom door, he was already smiling—lying in the exact same position as he'd started the night all those endless hours before.

"Can you freeze him?" he mouthed.

She nodded and fluttered her hands.

The child's body locked down in a sleeping paralysis—encased in the gentle hold of her magical spell. Gabriel extracted his arm from beneath him, sliding it carefully free, before laying him back down on the blankets and pressing a tender kiss to his cheek.

The ink lifted and the boy let out a quiet breath.

Sleep tight.

He pushed lightly to his feet and ghosted to the door—pressing it carefully shut, as he and Rae drifted down the hall. She threw him a secret glance, studying the side of his face.

"Are you okay?"

"My arm's asleep," he replied, stretching it out with a yawn. "How do people do this without training? How do they do it without superpowers?"

"Sometimes, people can't even do it with superpowers," she answered wisely, thinking back to many sacrificed extremities of her own. "Just ask me and my husband."

"Don't say the words *my husband* in this house."

She rolled her eyes with a smile. "You realize you're about to get married, right?"

He flashed a grin. "Old habit."

They reached the kitchen and he headed straight for the coffee-maker before remembering who he was speaking with and circling right back around. His hand flashed expectantly out as she conjured a strong cup of espresso—adding just the slightest hint of vanilla, the way he liked.

"You're a godsend," he murmured, inhaling the steam.

She waited as he took a long drink, continuing that silent assessment. "Seriously...are you doing okay?"

At that point, he honestly didn't know to what she was referring. The catastrophic mission with her husband, the heartbreaking rejection from his newly-adopted son, or the fact that he was officially getting married in just a few days' time. As it turned out, it was much simpler than that.

"Aria told me about the fight at school," she prompted quietly, relieved beyond words that the building was still standing. "Not the details or anything—just stupid jokes. Kids being kids."

I like jokes. Give me their names.

"Yeah, I'm doing okay," he answered, casting a reflexive glance up the hall. "Things are a little better, I think. At the very least, they're getting onto the right track."

She nodded solemnly. "They say gardening has that effect on people."

He burst out laughing, feeling better in spite of himself. She'd always been able to do that, find the thing he'd been missing. Say the exact words that he needed to hear.

"Devon thought I was planting handguns."

She laughed as well, sweeping back her long hair. "We all thought you were planting handguns. Devon *still* thinks that. I'm sure he'll be out there with a metal detector, searching for them in the dead of night." She paused a moment, then added. "Good thing he still has a hand. Otherwise, he'd never be able to hold it."

Gabriel stiffened abruptly, his fingers curling around the mug.

The friends didn't often call each other out for that sort of thing. They were good at what they did, they loved each other more than sunlight, and there was a general assumption that in such moments, each of them would assess the situation and make the best decision that they could.

But Gabriel wasn't exactly known for making rational decisions.

And he'd found out a second earlier about the bomb.

"Have you come here to kill me, then?" he asked quietly, glancing at her over the rim of his coffee. "Is this a final drink?"

She flashed a sweet smile. "Honey, it's what I put *in* the drink."

He stared into the cup, then set it down on the table.

Ironically enough, she wasn't asking for an apology. Despite having swept up the stuffing when her husband tore through their punching bag, she wasn't even asking to hear his side. She was simply bringing it to attention. They did that for each other. They'd done it for many years.

"I'm sorry about Devon," he said abruptly, surprising them both. "After the guy told me about the explosive, I was only going to arrest him. But then he lunged, and I just...reacted."

She stared at him in silence before conjuring a coffee for herself.

"I know," she replied simply. "Devon's a grown-up. He can take care of himself." She gave him a playful nudge. "It's *you* I need to look out for."

He chuckled, bowing his head.

I guess I deserve that.

They stood in silence for a while longer, leaning against the counter, staring out the window, sipping their drinks as the sun lifted slowly into the sky.

Acclimation, that was what Rae called it.

They'd done it a lot in the beginning—when he was still living in his apartment, before he and Natasha had moved into the house. Despite the utopic setting, it had been a difficult transition from what he'd been used to. He would wake up each morning and feel open to incursion, overly exposed. His brightly-lit bedroom was a far cry from the dark embrace of the cave. The air felt too thin, the windows felt too large. The sun itself felt too close, shining down without a filter.

She had come over for coffee every morning.

They didn't address it directly. Sometimes, they didn't even talk. They just sipped their drinks in silence, standing shoulder to shoulder, watching the rise of a new day.

"Barnes sent a message to Carter," she said quietly. "He wants to meet."

Gabriel stood there a moment, then turned slowly to face her. "Why the hell didn't you start with that?"

"I'm unpredictable."

"*Rae*—"

"Because we do this stuff first, Gabriel," she interrupted, clinking their mugs together before gesturing down the hall. "Because we don't put our lives on hold every time some new supervillain decides to tear the world apart. We make priorities. We stick to them." She finished her coffee and slung a purse over her shoulder. "Besides, I'm on my way to Carter's office right now."

The rest of the friends might have restrained themselves, lingering behind those professional boundaries until the president came to a decision himself, but those lines had blurred when it came to his stepdaughter, and Rae Kerrigan had never been known for her restraint.

Gabriel nodded swiftly, downing the rest of his cup. "I'm coming with you—"

"*You* have an appointment." Her eyes twinkled, as she pressed an immovable finger into his chest. "You're sampling cakes today, remember?"

He took a second to process the words, then let out a quiet sigh. Suddenly, the heaps of wedding paraphernalia stacked around his house felt more oppressive than anything else.

I wish I was in my garden.

His lips pursed with a frown.

Who the hell am I?

"Sampling cakes," he muttered, shaking his head. When he saw that she was still staring, he flashed a saccharine smile. "Priorities, right?"

She vanished out the door with a wink. "That's right."

THE CAKE-TASTING TURNED out to be a perfect continuation of everything else having to do with Gabriel and Natasha's wedding. They held each other's hands and did it together. Along with Molly.

"...this one tends to be a little sweeter than the Pralinsko..."

Gabriel let out a quiet breath, as yet another gourmet confection appeared on a porcelain platter for him to try. A sea of half-eaten samples already littered the table in front of them. Even Molly appeared to have lifted her ban on carbohydrates in order to sample each one.

He suspected this had a lot to do with their self-appointed guru.

The man had adorned himself with a cummerbund and a riding jacket, along with a dubious French accent. He laughed in a falsetto, cringed at the sound of passing traffic, and whistled the theme of *Masterpiece Theatre* as he told them everything there was to know about the world of lavish cakes.

Barnaby Cogsmith was his name.

There was a chance he was related to the concierge at Julian's haunted hotel.

"What do you think?"

Gabriel glanced up as Molly kicked him under the table. He stared blankly for a second, trying to rouse himself, before catching her dangerous expression and taking a bite of the cake.

"It's, uh…it's sweet."

Just like the last one. And the one before.

The man regarded him a moment, then snapped his fingers for another. "Let's talk about the strawberry bagatelle," he suggested lightly. "Now, usually I wouldn't push this kind of thing with a summer wedding, but in terms of holding the shape—"

"Why is it pink?" Gabriel interrupted, turning it over with his fork.

Barnaby stiffened as if that was a very stupid question.

"It's flavored with champagne," Molly hissed under her breath.

And the champagne is pink?

He nodded quickly. "Right."

For almost two hours, they'd been sitting in the stuffy parlor—listening to an endless stream of anecdotes, and getting a contact high from the sugary fumes. Gabriel could no longer remember what it was like in the outside world. There was a chance the day of the wedding had already come and passed. But what good were his decades of training, if they couldn't help him with something like this? He closed his eyes briefly, then leaned into it—forcing his attention back on the little man.

"The almond meringue and white chocolate mousse are other suitable options," Barnaby was saying, ticking them off on his hands. "And of course, you can never go wrong with tiramisu—"

"It can't be tiramisu," Gabriel interjected suddenly.

The others turned to him at the same time.

"You wouldn't like to—"

"It can't be tiramisu."

The man lifted his eyebrows as an awkward silence fell over the room. After it stretched on for a few seconds, he very ostentatiously scratched something off his list. "Alright—moving on."

Gabriel waited as the others watched him.

Barnaby cleared his throat and started again. "Not only does the cake set the tone for the entire reception, but it also says a lot of about the kind of couple you are as well. The kinds of choices you'll make, the amount of effort you'll put into maintaining the relationship." He took off his glasses, polishing them with a laugh. "I once predicted the birth of a couple's first child down to the month, because they went with the raspberry mousse."

...what the hell is happening right now?

Gabriel cast a quick look to the side, only to find he was completely alone in his confounded assessment. Molly was nodding fervently beside him. Even Natasha was bobbing her head.

A strange prickling started at the base of his neck, and he pushed suddenly from the table.

"Is there a restroom?"

Barnaby blinked up at him in surprise. "Down the hall, on your left."

He excused himself quickly and casually fled the little parlor, loosening the collar of his shirt, as he pushed open the door. The bathroom was cool and well-ventilated, providing a brief respite from the saccharine cloud that hung above the rest of the bakery. He cracked a well-used window, ran some cold water over his wrists, then looked up slowly at his own reflection.

You're having a panic attack. Calm down.

The door opened behind him.

"How ya doing?"

He leaned his head against the mirror as Natasha waltzed up behind him—giving him a quick kiss on the cheek. She hopped onto the counter a second later, swinging her legs.

"You're so American," he groaned.

How am I marrying an American?

She flashed a grin and pulled a pair of wireless earbuds from her hair.

She might not have spent decades working in covert intelligence, but she *had* spent countless hours being lectured by egotistical ballet instructors. Bobbing one's head to music looked a hell of a lot like nodding to the untrained eye. She stuffed them into her pocket, studying his face.

"You want to get out of here?"

"We can't," he said helplessly. "We need to find the perfect cake."

She smiled again, scooting over until she was in front of him. "I have an idea...what if we baked me *into* a cake?" Her eyes lit up at the prospect. "I could spring out at the appropriate moment. We should at least ask Barnaby what he thinks."

Gabriel stared at her a moment, then bowed his head with a smile. "Yeah, that sounds perfect."

A slender hand slipped into his own. "This is nothing I need, Gabriel. All of this wedding stuff...I was just doing it for you."

He blinked, looking down at her. "I was just doing it for *you*."

There was a pause.

"Well, now we *both* have to do it for Molly."

He chuckled under his breath. "Agreed."

The dizziness passed and the prickling in his neck subsided. Slowly but surely, the world stopped its manic spinning and steadied back into view.

"We still have to pick something," he murmured dispiritedly.

I like chocolate, he almost said. But he was suddenly afraid that might be wrong.

"If we go with the lemon meringue, we'll get divorced within the first year. If we go with the strawberry bagatelle, we'll end up with sixteen children and a moat."

He shook his head helplessly, leaving it in her hands. "What do you think?"

She hopped off the counter with a shrug. "Whatever you like best. I don't like cake."

AFTER ANOTHER TWENTY minutes picking his way through various shades of fondant, Gabriel finally did the sensible thing and called in a bomb threat to the bakery. While there was a good chance by her expression that Molly suspected what he'd done, the friends poured onto the street with the rest of them, and he managed to make it into his car not long after that.

Only an hour later, he was breezing into the Oratory.

A series of frantic shouts echoed off the ceiling, and the aroma of sweat and blood hit him at the same time. There was a fire brewing unattended in one corner, a tiger grooming itself in another.

Much better.

He shrugged out of his jacket, tossing it onto the floor.

"Hey, Alden—I thought you were banned until the big day!"

As Gabriel had come to realize, there were very few places on the planet where the reach of Molly Skye did not extend. Upon having determined that she was unable to control everything the groom would do until the wedding, she'd decided to control the people around him instead.

His training schedule had been mysteriously erased.

His fellow agents had been told to avoid him upon pain of death.

"I escaped," he called back, knotting back his golden hair. Molly had attempted to regulate that as well, booking him an appointment at an upscale salon. That had been the first of the bomb threats. The bakery had been the second. "You guys want to spar?"

The pair of agents who'd gotten his attention shared a quick look, then shook their heads with an unapologetic smile. Even if they were willing to risk Molly's wrath, they didn't much fancy being scraped across the floor by the likes of Gabriel Alden. They did, however, have a lot of both excited and unwanted questions about the big day.

"So have you picked out a song yet?" one of them asked, jogging lightly across the mats to join him. Having just been married himself, the checklists were all fresh in his mind. "For the first dance, I mean.

Vanessa wanted something classical, but we ended up going with Prince."

Interesting choice.

"Uh...no," Gabriel replied, shaking out his arms. "We haven't picked out a song."

"What about the booze?" the other inquired. "Have you finalized everything with the caterers? I heard this story last year about this couple who forgot to get a city permit. They were halfway through the appetizers, when the local precinct busted in and shut the whole thing down."

That prickling was back, inching its way up Gabriel's skull.

"Are you sure you don't want to spar?" he asked a little breathlessly. "I could really use the distraction—"

"What about the guy with the swans?" the first one laughed, nudging his partner. "Do you remember that? Tell him, Nathanial. You tell it way better than me."

The man cleared his throat with a grin. "It all started with this freak hailstorm—"

"Actually, can you hang on for a second?" Gabriel interrupted suddenly. "I forgot something in my locker."

"Yeah, of course."

The men continued sparring with each other as he jogged quickly across the practice mats and vanished into the hall. He paused there a moment, leaning back against the doors. The world had started spinning again, and his nails found their way sharply into his palms.

He grimaced, but leaned in to the pain. Then he made a split-second decision.

A second later, he headed for the locker room after all.

In a rare stroke of luck, the room was basically deserted. The only other person was a middle-aged demolitions expert who was sitting under the faucet of the shower and clearly wanted to be left alone. Gabriel cast another quick look around before opening the deadbolt on his locker with a sweep of his hand, and reaching towards a small pouch at the very back.

It crackled with age, but felt distressingly familiar to the touch. For more years than he cared to remember, his fingers could find the little seam to open it—even in the shadows, even as he slept.

He reached inside quickly, pulled out a bottle, and shook two pills into the palm of his hand. Another disturbing familiarity. But this one brought with it a sense of relief. And *profound* guilt.

Only this once. Only to get you to the wedding.

He let out a breath.

Then you can throw them away—

"Did you pick a cake?"

He jumped a mile, closing his fingers and whipping around, only to find his sister standing in the doorway. How long she'd been standing there was another question, but judging by the stiff set to her shoulders, he guessed it was long enough to have a pretty good idea what was going on.

Sure enough, she paced forward and caught his wrist, taking the pills from his hand.

"I thought you stopped taking these."

His pulse spiked and his cheeks flushed. "I did," he stammered. "I mean—I have. It's just...things have been getting harder, the closer we get to the wedding. I haven't been able to sleep."

She regarded him in silence.

It wasn't the first time they'd had such a conversation. The reason the pills had been hidden in the first place was because the last time she'd caught him taking them, she'd started taking them herself, one after another, despite his screaming protests, until he promised to throw them away.

He expected her to be angry. An older version of his fiery little sister might have stuck him with a knife. But she merely crushed them to a powder, dusting it calmly on her jeans.

"Plenty of other things to help you sleep."

He let out a slow breath. "...like what?"

She had such strange habits as it stood, he almost didn't want to ask about her coping techniques. But even when the ground beneath her was shifting, his sister had managed to find something steady. He had always admired that. He had always wished for it himself.

"Julian and I have a sexual arrangement."

He let out a burst of laughter, shaking his head. "I don't think he'd do that for me."

"I take deep breaths," she said calmly, having yet to crack a smile. "I stand by a window, put my face in the sun. Remind myself that I'm not in a tunnel, that I live somewhere with a sky." She tilted her head, staring up at him. "I call my brother," she finished softly.

Gabriel bowed his head, still flushed with a hint of shame. "Oh yeah? What does he say?"

She tossed back her hair with a shrug. "He doesn't have time for me anymore. He's about to get married."

The tension lifted and they shared a fleeting smile.

"About that," Gabriel began hesitantly, trying not to act as worried as he felt. "Do we still think it's a good idea? I'm kind of a menace. We might have underestimated how *much* of a menace."

Angel flashed a grin. "Natasha needs a good menacing. And Jason's life has been roses, thus far," she added with a trace of dry sarcasm. "Time to stir in a bit of trouble."

For one of the first times ever, his little sister missed the mark.

Gabriel's smile faded, as he stared vacantly towards the hallway. It was quiet for the most part, but every so often, it would shatter with the ring of a cellphone, or the sudden burst of a laugh.

"I'm not sure if he wants me to do this," he murmured, wishing with all his heart that it wasn't true. "I'm not sure if I *can* do this. These people, Angie...they're *good* people. And they've been hurt," he added suddenly. "Maybe it's not...maybe they need someone better than me."

It was quiet for a very long time.

Then Angel reached into his locker and took out the pills.

"Do you know why you started taking these, and I never did?"

He wanted to make a joke about having a modicum of self-control, but that didn't really apply to Angel. At any rate, she wasn't joking. He'd never seen that particular look on her face.

"Because I had you," she answered softly. "These people don't need you to be perfect, Gabriel. They don't need you to be something different than what you are. They just need you to keep showing up. The way you always do. The way you always did for me."

In a move that surprised them both, she stretched onto her toes and gave him a sudden kiss on the cheek—tossing the pills into the trash a second later.

"And you can't do that if you're asleep."

It was an abruptly tender moment, the kind that the siblings would have scorned in other people, but had always felt very natural with each other. Instead of shying away with a joke or a deflection, they leaned into it—standing close together, holding each other's hands. He was about to suggest they blow off the training session entirely and grab some food in the city—when a sudden commotion at the end of the hallway made both of them turn their heads at the same time.

They shared a quick look, then started moving.

It wasn't just the initial burst of noise, it was the slow-building tension that followed. It swelled around them, like the buzzing of the hive, so that by the time they pushed open the double-doors, the Oratory was a very different place than they'd just left.

Angel froze in silence as Gabriel grabbed the arm of a passing shifter.

"What's going on?" he demanded. "What just happened?"

The man cast a dark look towards the entrance before pulling himself free.

"Carter made a decision about Barnes," he said roughly, storming towards the lockers himself. "He's letting him come back."

Chapter 13

By the time Carter actually called the meeting, the announcement had already leaked and his decision had been made clear. Even so, there were plenty of people with a *lot* to say about it.

"—but he's *attacked* people," Alicia was saying, having stitched up some of those people herself. "The man actually *attacked* our people, and you're letting him come back inside."

The young doctor usually didn't speak at such meetings. Her work at the hospital kept her so busy, she usually didn't even attend. But this wasn't a matter of agency housekeeping or operational logistics, it was an existential crisis—one that had torn a rift in the heart of the entire supernatural community. One that could hurt them still further. One that affected them all.

It was a slow-moving disaster, playing out in real time. No one knew how it had escalated so quickly. And no one knew who was on the right side.

Which is exactly what Barnes is after. This is playing right into his hands.

"Cliff has assured me he was in no way connected to the attacks on our people," Carter replied, raising his voice a little to be heard. "It was a radical faction of his supporters that was *fiercely* condemned and has already been dealt with. He assured me of this. You can trust it to be true."

Now it was Cliff again. Yesterday, it was 'that maniac who ripped my agency in half and is going to end up on a roasting spit in my back-yard.' Still, his words carried an undeniable weight.

"That's bull," Devon muttered under his breath, speaking only to Julian. The two were standing where they always did near the back, watching the mayhem unfold. "There are ways of getting around Carter's tatù. No one knows that better than Barnes."

It was an excellent point, though he kept it to himself. As strongly as he might object to Carter's decision, he would never voice such dissent aloud. Not once the call had already been made.

Other people didn't share those compunctions.

"I can't believe you're doing this," Rae muttered, lowering her voice still further with a vehement glare. "I thought we settled the matter this morning over scones."

Carter's eyes closed ever so briefly. "As I tried to *explain* to you this morning, my breakfast table is not the place where such decisions are made. Nor is it acceptable for you to break into my kitchen and proceed to announce your misgivings at a decibel that most assuredly carried beyond the parameters of the house."

Rae jutted up her chin in defiance. "Tell that to my mother. She made the scones."

Family squabbling aside, she certainly wasn't the only person who carried those misgivings, and agents of the Privy Council weren't generally known to keep those hesitations to themselves.

"My case manager left," a man called out from the back of the group, a tangle of shadows writhing like snakes across his hands. "That's my only contact when I'm on assignment, the person I'm supposed to trust most in the field. How am I supposed to put my life in someone's hands—"

"Like you ever call your case manager, anyway," Carter snapped in exasperation. "When you get in trouble in the field, you call *Sebastian* and everyone knows it."

There was a reluctant murmur of assent.

"Now listen, everyone...I appreciate the discussion and I appreciate the concern, but I am your elected president and this is the decision that I've made." His eyes swept around the room, softening a little as they rested upon each face. "I understand your misgivings," he continued quietly, "*trust* me, I share a great many of those misgivings myself. But we don't have a choice. The man left with half our agency. People you know, people you care about as much as I do myself. This isn't a question of operational logistics, this is a matter of community. Our community. And I'm not going to be the man who allowed *half* of our people defect into Canada because we couldn't settle a bloody agreement." Carter loosened his tie and stuffed his hands into his pockets.

A few heads snapped up with interest, Gabriel's included.

"Yes, that's where they've been staying," Carter said plainly. "Cliff admitted it freely. He also said it was a rash decision and he regrets it. He said a great many of them want to come back."

This made more of an impact.

Whatever hesitations people might have, however much they might want to hop on a plane and start a covert war with the Canadian National Guard, more than anything...they were hurt.

These were their people. These were their friends.

And if those friends wanted to come back...?

"The decision is final," Carter concluded abruptly. "And this meeting is finished."

He left without another word, leaving a sea of restless people in his wake.

It was quiet for only a few seconds before the discussions broke out in earnest. Only this time, the anger wasn't as universal as it was before. While most people in the room were willing to accept Carter's judgment just because he was the one who made it, some of the others were actually starting to agree. A few of those were starting to get excited. It had been weeks since the ground had shifted beneath them. Maybe things could start getting back to normal. Maybe they could get back to their lives, stop racing to cover lost ground. Maybe they could start making plans.

"Well, that was a dumpster fire if ever I saw one." Molly threw a sharp glance towards the door Carter had used to make his escape. "I'm thinking of rescinding his invitation." Those sharp eyes found Gabriel a moment later, narrowing a little more. "Maybe we could just *bomb* his house."

He stepped discreetly to the other side of Angel.

"The guy left him very little room to maneuver and he's doing the best he can," Devon answered, sounding profoundly tired. "But yeah...it's a nightmare. I can't believe he said yes."

The others merely stared in silence, watching the news sweep around the room. Julian had a hand resting on Rae's shoulder for balance—half in the present, half in the future.

"I guess we'll just deal with it after the wedding," Molly continued, pulling out an absurdly-sized day-planner and flipping towards the end. "At any rate, I don't see this happening until—*crap*!" She slammed the book shut, looking about two seconds away from tears. "I forgot to give him Beth's dress. The tailor called this morning and I've got it in the trunk of my car. There's no time to drive over there. I've got the caterers this evening, then the florist—"

"I'll do it," Gabriel said lightly, eager to make amends. "I can drop it by on my way home."

She looked up at him, eyes shining with tears. "Would you really? Because that would *really* help."

"It's no problem." He flicked her cheek with a quick smile, already pacing from the room. "I should do *something* to help with the wedding. I am the groom..."

GABRIEL RETRIEVED THE missing garment bag from the back of Molly's car, then made his way slowly back into the city, rolling to a stop alongside Carter's stately brownstone just as the sun began to dip lower in the sky. He was expecting to merely drop it off. A part of him was tempted to avoid all interaction and simply leave it by the door. But Carter opened it with a look of surprise.

"Gabriel, what are you doing here?"

He lifted the hanger on two fingers, flashing a tight smile. "This is for Beth. Molly forgot to give it to you after the meeting."

"Oh, right, right…" Carter took it automatically, folding it over his arm. They regarded each other a second, but just as Gabriel started backing away, he spoke up again. "Want to come inside?"

Gabriel froze on the porch, hands in his pockets. "Uh, yeah…sure."

The man beckoned him forward, and he stepped tentatively into the foyer—wiping his shoes on the mat, as the door swung shut behind him.

Over the years, he'd been to the house a thousand forgotten times. From kids' birthday parties, to backyard barbeques, to shared holidays wherein Beth would make homemade cider over a slow-burning fire. No matter how cold it got outside, the temperature was always perfect. No matter how many times the world started crumbling, everything was always immaculately set into place. At this point, courtesy of his training, he could probably sketch almost every room by memory.

But he could count on a single hand how many times he'd been into Carter's private office.

He followed the man down the hall, then paused hesitantly in the doorway—staring around with the same quiet reverence one might use in a library or a church. It looked exactly the same way he remembered—albeit with a new stack of Victorian fiction waiting to be read on the desk. Leather chairs, dark-stained wood, and a crystal decanter. Classical music was tinkling from the ceiling.

"Schubert," he remarked casually. "What's the occasion?"

Carter flashed a quick look over his shoulder, surprised that he recognized the composer. A second later, he remembered the man he was speaking with and wasn't surprised at all.

"It's supposed to be meditative," he answered, pacing towards the decanter. "Julian recommended it." He removed the decorative top. "Drink?"

Gabriel looked at him in surprise. "Sure, thanks."

He watched as the man poured generously into two glasses and pressed one into his hand. It was whiskey of some kind. The kind that smelled expensive, even from afar.

He took a polite sip, then made a concerted effort to control his face. "It's really good."

Carter's lips twitched with a wry smile. "It's terrible," he corrected plainly. "A gift from a well-meaning secretary." He took a sip for himself and shuddered. "I'm trying to use it up on other people."

They laughed quietly and sipped again without thinking—eyes tightening with the same painful grimace, before setting it back on the desk.

"Have a seat," Carter invited, gesturing to one of the fireside recliners. "Not like you have a million things to do before your wedding. How's the preparation going? Anything I can do to help?"

Gabriel shook his head with a smile. "Thanks, but I think between the conjurers and Molly, we've got it covered. The girl's a force of nature. You should make her wear an inhibitor at all times."

"I've tried that," Carter murmured, leaning back in his chair. "Is that boy of yours excited?"

Gabriel paused, caught unexpectedly off-guard. "I don't know," he admitted. "He's not really talking about it." He paused again, then added suddenly, "I think it might be a little too much."

Carter nodded slowly, gentling with a frown. "He's been through a lot for someone his age. For *any* age," he amended, tracing the rim of his glass. "But he wears it well. Not unlike someone else I know." His eyes twinkled in the dancing flames. "Keep giving him time. It'll work itself out."

Gabriel nodded in return, eyes on the desk.

What am I doing here?

"You were awfully quiet at the meeting today."

...there it is.

He shifted uncomfortably in his chair. "Yeah, well...the rest of you were pretty loud."

Carter regarded him intently, head tilted to the side. "You don't agree with my decision?" he asked quietly. When the assassin merely shrugged, he caught his eye. "That matters here, Gabriel. You don't agree with my decision? You think I shouldn't allow him to return?"

Gabriel hesitated a moment longer, then decided to jump in. "I think he's shown you who he is," he said frankly. "A man who can walk away with half your agency. A man whose agenda could destroy us all. I think his fingers are all over those attacks, I think he's always been jealous of your chair. And in spite of all that...you invited him to return."

Carter's eyes tightened around the edges, but he didn't look angry. "That's half our people, Gabriel. I was being lenient—"

"You were being proud. You don't want the legacy of it. You don't want the split." He leaned forward, holding the man's gaze. "You didn't *cause* the split. But you can stem the bleeding."

The men stared at each other in silence, then reached at the same time for the whiskey. They remembered at the last second, placing it casually back on the desk.

"What would you suggest?"

"I don't know." Gabriel leaned back with a sigh, raking back his hair. "I'd probably re-frame the scope of mission assignments and prioritize them in terms of greatest loss of life—humanitarian efforts, medical research, acts of genocide. Forget everything corporate—inactive military targets, internal security. They can sweat it out like everyone else. I'd also scale back on caseloads, because agents shouldn't be sent into the field without a partner."

His voice sharpened with the slightest bit of an edge.

"You should know that better than anyone, Andrew. I spent a fair portion of my childhood sleeping next to Jacob Decker, listening to him scream. It *can't* be business as usual, the stakes you're playing with are too high." There was a pause. "I'd also fire Devon. To boost morale."

Carter leaned back in his recliner, watching him with a smile. "You know, if I was ever to retire...I sometimes think you and Devon would make a brilliant partnership to take over my chair. You have the perfect balance of perspectives."

Gabriel laughed humorlessly. "Yeah, because we've worked together so well in the past." His eyes flashed up with a sudden burst of nerves, thinking about their last mission. "Why *did* you pair us together? You made a spur of the moment decision about Weber, I get that. But you could have carried it out any time."

Carter regarded him in silence—one that stretched for so long, Gabriel was worried he'd crossed some invisible line. He shifted uncomfortably in his chair, dropping his gaze.

"You don't have to tell me—"

"We never really talked, after that night at the Abbey. When you gave me your hand."

Gabriel went abruptly still, tense to the point of breaking.

It had happened years ago, but he still remembered like it was that very day.

He had just revealed himself to have been working for Cromfield—a heartless assassin, who'd been sent with the specific purpose of infiltrating the council and destroying his stepdaughter's life. He'd done so in the house of her mother. He'd done so surrounded by a team of angry intelligence operatives who'd been supernaturally gifted to take his life.

But he didn't want to fight them anymore. He wanted to fight by their side. So he'd done the only thing he could think of—he'd rolled up his sleeve and offered Carter his hand.

It had been a turning point, one that had gone on to define his very future, by erasing everything that had come before. A casual gesture, but nothing about Carter's tatù was casual.

The man saw *everything*.

Every meal he'd ever eaten, every word he'd ever said. Every time Cromfield had beaten him, congratulated him. Every time he'd cried in the mirror after striking down an innocent target. Every time he'd had sex. A single touch, and the man knew it all. And he'd chosen to accept him.

"I went to visit an old friend of mine after," he continued quietly, "a man who dealt in memories, like Natasha. I needed someone to help me...balance the weight."

Gabriel's cheeks flushed, but he remained silent. He wasn't sure whether to apologize, or simply run screaming from the room. They might not have spoken since the night it had happened, but not a day had passed when he hadn't thought of it. In the days immediately after, he'd felt like he was being publicly unzipped and peeled open every time Carter happened to catch his gaze.

"There was one memory in particular, I was never able to forget." Carter's eyes clouded as he remembered, staring at the man in front of him, while seeing him at a younger age. "Cromfield had taken a prisoner, a hydrokinetic who was refusing to break. The two of you went down the tunnels one evening and opened the door, only to find they had drowned themselves."

Gabriel stifled a shudder, remembering the night himself.

"You opened the door and all this water flooded out," Carter said quietly. "The body floated out a moment later, it bumped into your knees. You couldn't have been more than six or seven, the same age Jason is right now. You didn't even scream. It's like he took that right out of you." His eyes tightened and softened at the same time. "That's when he told you...*clean it up.*"

A long silence stretched between them, one that neither was able to break. Gabriel's fists were balled so tightly, there was a chance he would fracture a finger. But Carter had gone oddly still.

"He couldn't break that boy, either," he said abruptly. "No one ever could. That boy grew up to be one of the finest agents in PC history. And one of the finest men I've ever known." His lips curved with a hint of pride. "That's why I paired you with Devon. Because men like that should stick together."

THE MEN FINISHED THEIR whiskey in silence, burning the inside of their throats, then Gabriel muttered something about having to get home to Natasha, and they headed out to the door.

"This was nice," Carter remarked, opening it with a smile, "we should do it again sometime."

Gabriel raked back his hair with a grin. "Drinking bad whiskey and talking about my tortured past?" He raised an eyebrow, slipping into his coat. "Yeah, let's definitely make a habit of it."

The headmaster chuckled as he stepped out the door. "Speaking of Devon," he continued suddenly, "we haven't gotten a chance to speak about your mission. That was quite the case report I read this morning."

Gabriel froze on the steps, his pulse quickening. "You read the case report?"

There was a case report?

Carter nodded slowly, staring at him all the while.

"It's a shame about Weber, but upon reading it, I have to say I was rather pleased. I've read a hundred of Devon's reports, but I've never seen such glowing praise. Either he wrote it with a gun to his head, or you did something to seriously impress him that day."

Gabriel hesitated a split second, then ventured out on a limb. "Let's say he was impressed."

Carter nodded with a twinkling smile. "Sure, let's go with that."

GABRIEL WAS INTENDING to drive home, but he ended up going somewhere different instead.

"Hey, buddy."

He sat cross-legged in the graveyard, propping his legs against the headstone, with a silver flask clutched loosely in his hands. Wyatt Gaines. The plot was immaculate as always, bursting with fresh flowers. That was all Angel. She came every week, though she'd never mentioned it.

Gabriel wouldn't mention it either.

"I'm getting married in a few days. A girl I met in New York. A tech nerd, a dancer. You'd like her." There was a pause. "You'd like her a little too much. I probably wouldn't introduce you."

He smiled at this. He imagined Wyatt was smiling as well.

"I also tanked a mission, I'm sure you'd like to hear about that. Carter sent me with that creep I was telling you about...who turned out to be a kind of decent guy." He traced his fingers in the grass, considering this with a thoughtful expression. "You'd say I pre-judged him. Which is really fucking ironic, considering how much fun you always had pre-judging people yourself."

He tried to smile again, then grew suddenly nervous.

"I adopted him, Wyatt. He's officially my son."

For almost two full years, he'd been waiting to say it. Now that it had finally happened, he couldn't seem to find the words. The funny thing was, it might have been Angel. She had offered, immediately. She had offered before she'd even spoken to Julian. And Angel didn't make offers the way other people did. She was fully prepared to see it through. Except her brother hadn't let her.

He'd taken the boy himself.

"He looks like you," he said softly, forcing a tight smile. "That's hard sometimes." His eyes swept over the headboard, imagining his friend's face. "I'll never understand why you never told me," he murmured.

"You're one of my best friends...how could you never tell me you had a son?"

A hundred times, he'd asked the question. He never got an answer.

He guessed he never would.

With a silent breath, he lifted the flask to his lips and took a long drink—thinking of all that had happened, thinking of all that was still to come. After a long while, he poured a shot for Wyatt.

Then he poured another.

"You'd want two."

WHEN GABRIEL FINALLY got home that evening, he was surprised to see the silhouette of a little boy sitting on the porch. He cut the engine and jogged quickly up the steps to join him.

"You're up late. More bad dreams?"

Jason shook his head, pushing slowly to his feet.

The bruise on his face had mostly faded, but beneath the overhanging porch light, Gabriel could still see a faint outline. He opened his mouth with the question, moved with a compulsion he could scarcely control. But he *did* control it. A second later, he flashed a tight smile.

"Want to head inside? I could make some hot chocolate—"

"Some kids at school were teasing me," Jason said abruptly. "They said that adoptions were fake and you guys just felt sorry for me. They said I didn't have a real father." He lifted his chin with a touch of defiance, fixing those blue eyes on Gabriel's face. "I told them I did."

For one of the first times in his life, Gabriel Alden didn't know what to say. He stood there in a kind of daze, startling slightly when the boy reached out to touch his sleeve.

"...could I still be your best man?"

A rush of feeling swept over him, so powerful, it couldn't be controlled. He drew in a deep breath, feeling it shiver all the way through him, before he nodded with a shining smile.

"I wouldn't want anyone else."

The two shared a smile, then walked slowly into the house—catching the windchimes at the same time so they wouldn't wake Natasha. They headed down the hallway, then turned off their separate ways, but a second before Jason could vanish into his room, Gabriel caught his arm.

"Why did you say no?" he asked quietly. "When I asked you the first time?"

The child froze a split second, then decided to tell the truth. "You and mom have both been so excited for the wedding, making all these plans to start something new..." He bit down on his lip, almost too scared to finish. "You didn't plan on me."

Gabriel took a single look at him, then seized him in an embrace.

It seemed like he'd been waiting all his life for that very moment. A *perfect* moment. The kind he never would have known to look for until he was staring into those beautiful blue eyes.

"I didn't plan on you," he whispered. "You took me by surprise."

Chapter 14

The next day started with a gift.

Gabriel casually kidnapped Molly from her penthouse at seven in the morning, and drove her to an upscale café. She chattered nonstop all the way across town—not noticing what they were doing, or where they were doing. Not even thinking it was very strange that she'd been kidnapped.

Then she glanced through the window and went dead still.

Breathe.

"Gabriel...that's Roberto Cavalli."

He nodded with a faint smile, staring at the side of her face. "We met a few years ago in Paris. I stood for a few fittings, helped him with his new line." If memory served, the man had gotten a little frisky, but that was water under the bridge. "I texted him last week, told him my wedding planner was a fan. The two of you are going to have a little chat."

She turned to him slowly, eyes as wide as saucers. "But how—"

He leaned across the car, pressing a gentle kiss to her cheek. "*Thank you*, Molly. This wedding...it means a lot."

It looked like she nodded, but there was a chance she was just shaking.

She got out of the car a second later, walking like a robot into the café. He watched through the dash as she approached the table, sinking into an awkward curtsy about halfway there.

He slipped on a pair of sunglasses, and drove away with a grin.

She doesn't even curtsy at the palace.

Things had devolved from there.

Julian threw him a bachelor party after all, but Angel had added a little twist. She convinced her husband and the rest of the groomsmen, it would have to be a surprise. She had done this after texting Gabriel to come over, allowing him to listen to his heart's delight.

"You'll have to kidnap him," she said flatly. "Otherwise, it doesn't count."

Julian's eyes flashed preemptively white, as Luke and Devon started nodding. A second later, the psychic came back pale from the future, and the rest of them froze at the same time.

"Wait...you want us to grab him?" Devon asked hesitantly. "Like—bash him over the head with something and stuff him in the trunk of my car?"

Luke nudged him with a grin. "Don't pretend you haven't thought about it."

Angel ignored them. "Yeah, that's pretty standard. I looked it up."

The men shared a quick look, then Julian was pushed forward.

"Honey," he began delicately, "that's a really sweet idea, but trying to kidnap someone with Gabriel's background...?" He trailed away uncertainly. "It might not turn out so well."

"He'll kill us," Luke clarified bluntly.

"And he'll break my car," Devon added with a shudder.

Angel stared at them a moment, going slowly down the line, then she folded her arms and rewarded each one with the most exquisite smile.

"You guys are the world's *top* superheroes," she said slowly. "You will have access to magic, you will have the element of surprise. You are tasked with apprehending just a single man."

There was a weighty pause.

"Are you telling me you can't handle something like that?"

It was a masterclass in manipulation. And it worked like a charm.

They laughed it off like a joke—scoffing all the while—then walked away to begin making their preparations, quickening their pace the second they were out of sight.

Gabriel waited until they were gone, then slipped out from behind the corner. "That was hilarious."

"It's only the first part of my present," Angel answered with a smile, sweeping back her long hair. "You'll get the second after the wedding."

The wedding.

After so many months of waiting...the day had almost arrived.

"I can't believe this is actually happening," he murmured.

She gave him an appraising look. "You want to back out?"

"No."

"You want me to confiscate your passport, stop you from fleeing the country?"

"Which passport?"

"I'm serious—"

"No," he interrupted with a smile. "I *want* this. It's not the wedding. It's Natasha." The smile faded into something more serious. "I want to be with her as long as I can."

Angel's eyes sparked with a little smile. "Then this is really happening."

Yeah, I guess it is.

They split off in opposite directions. One—to abduct a ballerina and take a last minute flight to Guam. The other—to sit in his living room and wait for his friends to assault him.

Just before they lost sight of each other, she called over her shoulder.

"Gabriel...act surprised."

THEN, ALL AT ONCE, the day had arrived.

Upon Molly's fierce insistence, everyone arrived almost two hours early to the venue. Since Natasha had no real preferences and Gabriel had refused to venture anywhere near a church, they'd settled on a breathtaking garden in a secluded part of the city. It had clearly been designed for such things, with a flowering archway and chairs, along with a tiny stone building in which the bride and groom could get ready. They were getting ready at that very moment. At least, they were trying.

"Alright, so I've got bridesmaids and groomsmen quartered off in the eastern and northern wings respectively, while the rest of you need to stick to either the garden or veranda to enjoy your cocktails and stay the hell out of the way." Molly was perched halfway up the stone steps, barking out orders like a seasoned general. "Luke, go back to our car and find that box of extra champagne flutes I told you we didn't need to pack. Aria—spit that out of your mouth, it isn't candy. *Angel*!"

She raced forward as the girl swept past the flowers in a tailored suit, looking like she'd just stepped off the runway. There had been some last minute alterations that needed to be done, but after having what both of them would remember as a memorable chat, Mr. Cavalli had helped.

"This looks perfect," she breathed, giving the sleeves an extra tug. "Alright, so the rest of the groomsmen are getting set up in that stone building with the weird roof, but as the best man, I'm actually going to need—"

"I've already got my best man."

The others looked up as Gabriel slipped an arm around Jason's shoulder. The boy shivered under their combined gaze, but straightened up—looking the faintest bit proud.

"Yeah, that's me."

The rest of the friends secretly melted. Molly went white as a sheet.

"Rae...?" she trilled in a panic.

The girl rushed forward, reaching for her trembling hand.

"It's okay, I've got this." She winked at Jason before gesturing Angel inside. "Come on, Decker. I'll conjure you a dress. You should get ready, too," she added, throwing an over-the-shoulder grin at Gabriel. "People will be arriving soon."

He nodded quickly, stomach fluttering with a sudden burst of nerves.

It's really happening.

He threw a swift glance at his groomsmen, all of whom were already dressed and pressed in a trio of impeccable suits. Julian caught his eye and smiled, tapping his temple. Yes—he'd already checked the future. And yes—everything turned out fine. Luke flashed him a quick thumbs-up, holding a writhing Benji under his arm, while Devon mouthed a clear, "Don't fuck it up."

Gabriel grinned, biting his lip. To be honest, he was surprised any of them were speaking to him. After the events of the previous evening, they were all bound to be feeling a little bit sore.

The bachelor party itself was the world's most spectacular and infantile fun.

Julian had taken him to play laser tag.

It was a joke they'd shared from those early days, after the dust had settled at the sugar factory and they were first getting to know each other. It had been a little difficult finding common ground. It had been even more difficult finding shared points of reference. When the psychic had mentioned the concept as a brief aside in a larger story, both he and Angel had tilted their heads at the same time. Laser tag? They'd never heard of it. He'd reflected a moment, then confessed it was very similar to the way they'd both grown up. When they'd pulled into the parking lot, Gabriel had doubled over at the waist—laughing so hard, it was a full ten minutes before he was able to stop.

The abduction itself was a different story.

Bless their hearts, the guys had given it their all.

Luke called him up with a crisis—his car had broken down and he'd been stranded along the side of the road. Then lo and behold—Devon and Julian showed up as well! The fox was actually holding a tire-iron, a sight that made Gabriel more than a little nervous, but the psychic had brought a cup of coffee. He offered it with a sweet smile, and they all stared with comical attention as he took the first sip. Flash forward a few minutes later, and their egos would never recover.

Neither would Devon's car.

He gave them all a comical salute, then headed up the stone walkway, only to stop almost immediately as a sudden hand caught him by the shoulder.

"Could I steal a quick word?"

He glanced back in surprise to see Carter standing behind him, wearing an impeccable suit of his own. Beth was standing just a few paces behind, bouncing James on her hip with a warm smile.

"Yeah, of course." He raked back his hair, feeling those nerves again.

So much had happened in the last twenty-four hours, there hadn't yet been time to process the strange conversation they'd shared over whiskey and firelight. It was of such a sensitive nature, he was suddenly worried he should have followed it up with a few quick words himself.

"I won't keep you," Carter said quickly, "I don't want to take any time away from the big day, except to tell you this. My father passed away before I married Beth. I always wondered what he would have thought of it, I always wondered what he might say. When I became a father myself, I stopped wondering those things, because the answer to both became quite clear."

He reached out between them, straightening Gabriel's collar. "I never got to know your father, I'll always wish that I had. But I can tell you with absolute certainty...he would be very proud."

Gabriel caught his breath, then nodded—his eyes fixed on the ground. A second later, he surprised them both, by pulling the man into a sudden embrace.

"Thank you," he murmured. "Thank you for saying that."

Carter warmed with a secret smile. "You've got this."

Molly appeared between them, looking like the devil herself. *"Get. Inside."*

They pulled apart with a nervous laugh, sharing a parting look, before heading off in separate directions. Carter relocated with the rest of the family into the garden, while Gabriel jogged up the stone steps and locked himself in a dressing room—one that was completely empty, save for a bottle of water, a bottle of whiskey, a bottle of mouthwash, and a long mirror.

"Alright," he breathed aloud, staring at his reflection, "you can do this..."

He got dressed quickly, running his fingers through his hair enough times that it fell in golden waves around the sides of his face. He briefly considered tying it back, but he wasn't sure if that was informal, and at any rate, he was afraid to do anything he hadn't cleared first with Molly.

He located his shoes and was just attempting the stubborn zipper on his pants, when the door pushed suddenly open and his little sister swept into the room.

His head snapped up in surprise.

"It was locked."

She twirled a delicate silver pin, sliding it back into her hair. "I wanted to check on you, make sure you weren't too deep into the whiskey." Her blue eyes flitted over, resting on the bottle in surprise. "But you haven't even touched it."

"Too nervous," he admitted, bouncing a little in place.

Her eyes warmed and she crossed the room to his side, calmly locating the buttons his frantic fingers had missed by mistake. "I wanted to thank you for reminding me about the latex kimono," she remarked off-handedly. "Turns out, they sell them in London. Jules and I had a little fun..."

His face tightened with a grimace. "Stop telling me things like that."

"Never." She finished with the shirt, then looked up at him appraisingly—measuring his expression the same way she'd done since she was a child. "You want a minute?"

He flashed a quick smile, shaking his head.

Like everything else about his sister, it wasn't a casual offer.

"Isn't that bad form?" he quipped. "To freeze people on your wedding day?"

Bad luck, maybe. They have all sorts of rules about weddings and luck.

She lifted her shoulders with a shrug. "I did."

He grinned in spite of himself, she most certainly had.

Angel had married Julian on a bridge in Florence, the same bridge where she'd been sent to intercept him all those years before. She'd bought the dress the day before and threaded her hair with soft flowers, stepping into the sunshine like the most beautiful thing he'd ever seen.

Then she saw Julian...and froze the entire city.

"How long did you keep that up?" he asked with a chuckle, having been the only person spared from the ink. They'd walked the city together, repositioning the tourists and making little changes to their heart's delight. "I never asked."

"Long enough for me to catch my breath."

She stepped forward suddenly, placing both hands on his shoulders.

"I'm going to say something now," she said quietly, "and there's a good chance you won't like it. But I need you to hear it all the same."

He stiffened beneath her palms. "...okay?"

She pulled in a breath, trying her best for a smile.

"I know we only remember the bad things—the things he made us say, the things he made us do. It's easy to only remember the bad things...but he would be proud."

There was a beat of silence.

"You are unbelievable." Gabriel shook his head with a low chuckle. "On my *wedding* day."

She kissed him on the cheek. "Knock 'em dead, big brother." She tossed back her hair and paced to the door. "If you forget your line, it's something like, I...?" She waved a hand dismissively. "It'll come to me."

"Get out."

The door swung shut behind her, as he turned back to his reflection—reconsidering his idea of sending weekly gift baskets to her therapist. The seats in the garden were slowly filling to capacity as they neared the appointed hour. Molly would be sending someone to retrieve him soon.

If I can just fix this bloody zipper—

"Room service."

He lifted his eyes, as the door opened once again and a dark-haired beauty sailed into the room. Having successfully conjured everything her best friend could think to ask, Rae had been sent to make sure the notoriously impulsive groom hadn't done anything stupid.

Like flee the country. Or forget to write his vows.

"Did Molly send you?" he asked, turning back to the pants. Despite his increasingly violent efforts, he was only managing to make the problem worse. Even his tatù was ineffective. Instead of unsnagging the metal, the edges had begun to melt. "She wants to make sure I'm still landlocked?"

Rae flashed a grin, hopping onto the counter. "Actually, I came to see if you needed any help with your vows."

My vows.

His face went still, before he made a deliberate effort to clear it.

"I don't have anything too formal," he said casually, angling around so there wasn't the slightest chance he could look her in the eyes. "I figured I'd get up there and speak from the heart."

She nodded slowly, not the slightest bit fooled. "And now?"

"...I think I broke my zipper."

She snorted with laughter, hopping down to see for herself. "You are such a child sometimes," she muttered, sinking to her knees for a better angle. "We shouldn't even allow you to get married. You should need to complete some remedial courses first."

He bounced nervously, glancing at the clock. "Could you just fix it?"

She was certainly trying, using a combination of a strength tatù and a bit of oil she conjured with a flick of her hands. "Crayons and zippers. No running by the pool. Maybe some blocks."

"You are *so bloody funny*," he answered scathingly, sliding them down his hips. "Just conjure me some new ones and make sure to replicate the tag. There's no reason Molly ever has to know—"

"Your *vows*, Gabriel." She looked up at him, leaning back on her heels. "What are you doing to say in your vows? Because trust me, that's not something you want to decide in the moment."

He stared down at her, feeling completely off-balanced.

"I don't know," he replied faintly, having torn himself to pieces over that very question for the last few weeks. "I don't know what to say. What *can* you say? She makes me want to get up in the morning. She makes me want to actually *live* my life. From a psychoanalytical perspective, she's probably the reason behind that whole fiasco with the garden, but I don't—" He caught himself in frustration, raking back his hair. "I don't know how to condense that into vows."

Most people would have laughed. Others might have reached for the whiskey. But Rae simply stared at him, a thoughtful expression settling into her eyes.

"Do you remember what you told me by the river?" she asked suddenly. "Right before we snuck into the palace, that week I accidently got us stuck back in time?"

We need to find better points of reference.

"You said that you wanted to be with her," she finished softly. "Some people complicate it, there are a thousand ways to complicate it. Lord knows the two of you haven't had the easiest story, but sometimes, it really is that simple. You want to be with her...in every way that you can."

Their eyes met, warming with a look of shared understanding.

"Now take off your pants. We don't have a lot of time—"

"I *knew* it!"

The door flew open a final time and Natasha appeared in the frame—looking like a creature sent down from heaven, pointing an accusatory finger directly at Gabriel's chest.

"I *knew* you still had feelings for her!"

He let out a gasp of panic and yanked up his pants, staggering away from Rae at the same time. "No, this isn't...she was just helping with my...sweetheart, I would never—"

Both girls burst out laughing as he stared in horror.

"This isn't funny!" he insisted, reaching for that whiskey after all. "Did you hear what I just said?! You're not supposed to hear that yet, Natasha! I'm not even supposed to be seeing you, for some reason. You look like a *dream*, by the way. Just...just erase this from your memory!"

There was a beat of silence.

"Did you do it?!"

The girls regarded him with the same tender smile.

"What a freak show," Rae muttered, shaking her head.

Natasha clapped her on the shoulder with a grin. "I can take it from here."

Rae slipped out of the room with a parting wink, as Natasha took her place—examining the mangled zipper, before somehow fixing the thing with a few quick twists of her finger.

Gabriel stared down in astonishment. "How did you...?"

"Ballerina," she said simply. "I know a thing or two about zippers."

They stood for a suspended moment, both feeling the magnitude of what was about to happen, before they came together without speaking—fitting into each other's arms.

"You never told me," she murmured against his shirt. "You never told me what made you change your mind. Abandon the dark side and try for something different."

He glanced down in surprise, staring at the top of her head.

"Let me add a quick side-note," she added, before he could speak. "In my head, it's always been something like: you looked down at Rae's perfect face and suddenly discovered the meaning of true love. So in the spirit of our wedding, if it was some *other* reason..."

He chuckled softly, tightening his grip.

"Did you just...believe in her?" she asked softly. "Believe in them?"

His breathing hitched, then steadied. "It had nothing to do with them."

She lifted her eyes in confusion. "But you always said—"

"I never said it was to do with them."

"But they always said—"

"*They* are the most arrogant people you will ever meet," he interrupted with a grin. "Even the humble ones. Olympic-level arrogance." He paused, suddenly thoughtful. "But they were happy. In spite of everything they'd seen, everything they'd been through...they had managed to be happy."

His eyes locked onto hers.

"I wanted to be happy, too."

They stared a moment, then she flashed a quick smile.

"So this is pretty self-serving."

He laughed under his breath, drawing her closer. "Entirely self-serving. If you like, I can perform the ceremony myself, just meet you at home."

She nodded silently, pressing against him once more.

They could hear it now—the wedding getting started. The clink of champagne flutes had been joined with the sudden tinkling of music. People were settling into their chairs.

"Do you know what Canary said to me the day we met?" he asked softly.

She glanced up at him in surprise, shaking her head. "We were standing outside your apartment in Brooklyn. I'd been shot the night before, I was still bleeding from the chest. She looked up at me with those batty old eyes and said, 'Gabriel, this is going to be the solution to all of your problems.'" He swept back her hair, eyes gentling with a tender smile. "Looks like she was right."

CONSIDERING HOW LONG they'd planned it, the wedding itself was a blur.

The air smelled of flowers. Natasha walked herself down the aisle.

Gabriel stood at the altar waiting for her, a silver rose tucked into his lapel. There was silver in her bouquet as well. Something old and something new—resurrected from the flower he'd made for her back in New York. That had been Jason's idea. He was standing beside the altar as well.

Holding his father's hand.

The reception was the world's best party.

If they were being technical, there was plenty that had gone wrong. Devon had been sent to handle a persistent car alarm. The doves Molly had acquired to release upon their exit had begun to mate. The couple never noticed. They danced the night away, seeing nothing but each other.

Gabriel had *never* been so happy.

"You ready to go?" Natasha finally asked.

The sun had set long hours before and the children were stacked in a sleeping pile beside the fountain. Jason was sleeping amongst them, his shimmering hair intertwined with the rest.

They had decided to forgo the usual honeymoon—they had already travelled the world, and there was plenty of time to take one later. They wanted to go home as a family instead.

Just the three of them.

"Yeah," Gabriel answered, drawing her close. "I'm ready."

Even as he said the words, his entire body seemed to thrill at the idea. In a split second of sheer bliss, he realized he wasn't ever as excited about the wedding, as he was for the morning after.

When that life he'd been craving actually started. When it was finally, *finally* his turn.

He glanced around and took one final mental picture.

His friends were still dancing. The music was still playing. There were plenty of empty seats and plenty of empty tables, but he wouldn't worry about that now.

For tonight, they'd have the fairytale. For tonight, happily ever after was enough.

THE NEXT MORNING, GABRIEL rose with the dawn.

With an uncontrollable smile, he picked himself out of bed and padded down the hall to the kitchen. Jason and Natasha were already gathered around the stove making pancakes. *Attempting* to make pancakes. There was music playing in the background. Every so often, she'd forget what they were doing and scoop him off his feet—spinning him around for a breathless dance.

Their laughter echoed off the ceiling. The pancakes were burning.

He drew in a deep breath, then stepped inside to join them.

The wisteria was dancing outside the window. Coming into bloom.

THE END

Not all sins can be forgiven.

Turn the page to see the ALMOST-COVER Rae had... you'll have to let me know which you like better!

WJ May

Ps... check out the next Chronicles of Kerrigan series that's coming this Autumn!!

KERRIGAN MEMOIRS #6
Chronicles
OF RAE
USA Today Bestselling Author
W.J. MAY

Kerrigan Presidents Series

"No man is an island..."

They said no man could ever replace Andrew Carter. So when he decided to take a step back from the Privy Council, he wasn't replaced by a single man. He was replaced by two.

Devon Wardell and Gabriel Alden never had the easiest relationship.

What started as teenage squabbles over the same girl, escalated into a supernatural blood-feud that grew infinitely more difficult when they became lifelong friends and their families moved in next door. After their children got married, they resolved to destroy each other once and for all.

But as usual, fate has other plans...

Leaders in Control
Director on a Mission
Devon Seeking Guidance
Gabriel Vanishing Light
President on Edge
Agreeing the Future

JULIAN'S COVER QUESTION

There is a reason why the cover is unique for "Julian" than what readers expected. You'll have to read Julian's story to find out why. However, I wanted to share a sneak peek into the original cover so readers can have some fun and try to figure out what's going on. Join me on my FB page, fan page or Instagram for clues and comments to be included in the conversation!

Here's the peek at the original cover... (one more page turn lol)

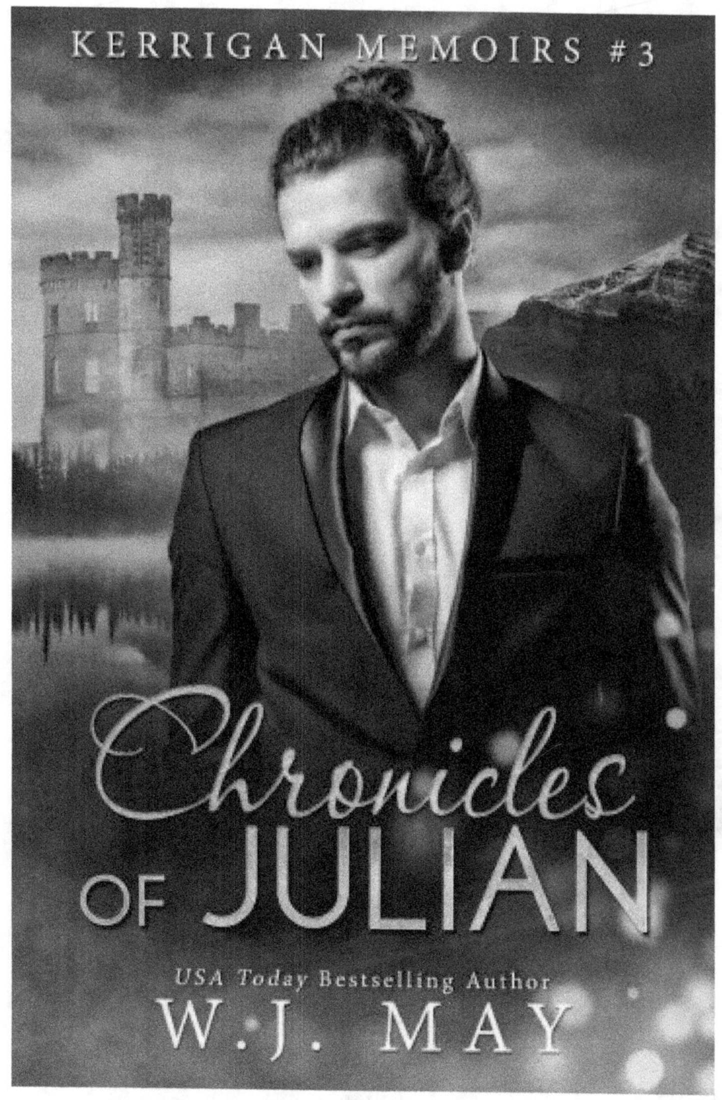
KERRIGAN MEMOIRS #3
Chronicles
OF JULIAN
USA Today Bestselling Author
W.J. MAY

The Chronicles of:

Devon

Angel

Julian

Molly

Gabriel

Rae

The Kerrigan Kids Series

Book 1 - School of Potential

Book 2 - Myths & Magic

Book 3 - Kith & Kin

Book 4 - Playing With Power

Book 5 - Line of Ancestry

Book 6 - Descent of Hope

Book 7 – Illusion of Shadows

Book 8 – Frozen by the Future

Book 9 – Guilt of My Past

Book 10 – Demise of Magic

Book 11- Rise of the Prophecy
Book 12 – Deafened by the Past

TUDOR COMPARISON:

Aumbry Hall –A recess to hold sacred vessels, often found in castle chapels.

Aumbry House was considered very special to hold the female students - their sacred vessels (especially Rae Kerrigan).

Joist Hall – A timber stretched from wall-to-wall to support floorboards.

Joist House was considered a building of support where the male students could support and help each other.

Oratory –A private chapel in a house.

Private education room in the school where the students were able to practice their gifting and improve their skills. Also used as a banquet - dance hall when needed.

Oriel –A projecting window in a wall; originally a form of porch, often of wood. The original bay windows of the Tudor period. Guilder College majority of windows were oriel.

Rae often felt her life was being watching through one of these windows. Hence the constant reference to them.

Refectory –A communal dining hall. Same termed used in Tudor times.

Scriptorium –A Medieval writing room in which scrolls were also housed.

Used for English classes and still store some of the older books from the Tudor reign (regarding tatùs).

Privy Council –Secret council and "arm of the government" similar to the CIA, etc.... In Tudor times, the Privy Council was King Henry's board of advisors and helped run the country.

Find W.J. May

Website:
https://www.wjmaybooks.com
Facebook:
https://www.facebook.com/pages/Author-WJ-May-FAN-PAGE/
141170442608149
Newsletter:
SIGN UP FOR W.J. May's Newsletter to find out about new releases, updates, cover
reveals and even freebies!
http://www.wjmaybooks.com/subscribe

The Chronicles of Kerrigan

Book I - *Rae of Hope* is FREE!
   Book Trailer:
http://www.youtube.com/watch?v=gILAwXxx8MU
Book II - *Dark Nebula*
Book Trailer:
http://www.youtube.com/watch?v=Ca24STi_bFM
Book III - *House of Cards*
Book IV - *Royal Tea*
Book V - *Under Fire*
Book VI - *End in Sight*
Book VII – *Hidden Darkness*
Book VIII – *Twisted Together*
Book IX – *Mark of Fate*
Book X – *Strength & Power*
Book XI – *Last One Standing*
BOOK XII – *Rae of Light*

PREQUEL –

Christmas Before the Magic
Question the Darkness
Into the Darkness
Fight the Darkness
Alone the Darkness
Lost the Darkness

W.J. May
THE CHRONICLES OF KERRIGAN SEQUEL
W.J. May
OF TIME
W.J. May
TIME PIECE
W.J. May
Second CHANCE
W.J. May
Glitch IN TIME
W.J. May
Our TIME
W.J. May
Precious TIME

SEQUEL –

Matter of Time
Time Piece
Second Chance
Glitch in Time
Out Time
Precious Time

The Chronicles of Kerrigan: Gabriel

Living in the Past

Present for Today

Staring at the Future

More books by W.J. May

Hidden Secrets Saga:
Download Seventh Mark part 1 For FREE
Book Trailer:
http://www.youtube.com/watch?v=Y-_vVYC1gvo

LIKE MOST TEENAGERS, Rouge is trying to figure out who she is and what she wants to be. With little knowledge about her past, she has questions but has never tried to find the answers. Everything changes when she befriends a strangely intoxicating family. Siblings Grace and Michael, appear to have secrets which seem connected to Rouge. Her hunch is confirmed when a horrible incident occurs at an outdoor party. Rouge may be the only one who can find the answer.

An ancient journal, a Sioghra necklace and a special mark force life-altering decisions for a girl who grew up unprepared to fight for her life or others.

All secrets have a cost and Rouge's determination to find the truth can only lead to trouble...or something even more sinister.

Don't miss out!

Visit the website below and you can sign up to receive emails whenever W.J. May publishes a new book. There's no charge and no obligation.

https://books2read.com/r/B-A-SSF-NWSYB

BOOKS2READ

Connecting independent readers to independent writers.

Did you love *Chronicles of Gabriel*? Then you should read *Living in the Past*[1] by W.J. May!

The past is your lesson. The present is your gift. The future is your motivation.

From USA Today bestselling author, W.J. May brings you a spin off from the Chronicles of Kerrigan. This is a stand alone series, or can be read with the Chronicles of Kerrigan series

How can you build a future, when a part of you is trapped in the past?

Gabriel Alden's problems were supposed to be over. The man who had enslaved him had been destroyed. The girl he was supposed to kill, had become his saving grace. And the people he had been sent to in-

---

1. https://books2read.com/u/bzpMAz

2. https://books2read.com/u/bzpMAz

filtrate, had ended up as family. So why, when everyone else had found their happy-ever-after, was Gabriel still out in the cold?

Dark memories, hidden shadows, and secrets too terrible to imagine haunt his every breath—chasing after him as he races around the globe, searching for the truth.

Can he ever truly escape his past? Will he ever have a shot at a future? How far can you run before your ghosts finally catch up with you?

One thing is certain, Gabriel's problems are just getting started...

The Chronicles of Kerrigan: GabrielLiving in the PastPresent for TodayStaring at the Future

READ THE WHOLE SERIES:Prequel Series:Christmas Before the MagicQuestion the DarknessInto the DarknessFight the DarknessAlone in the DarknessLost in Darkness

The Chronicles of Kerrigan SeriesRae of HopeDark Nebula-House of CardsRoyal TeaUnder FireEnd in SightHidden DarknessTwisted TogetherMark of FateStrength & PowerLast One StandingRae of Light

The Chronicles of Kerrigan SequelA Matter of TimeTime PieceSecond ChanceGlitch in TimeOur TimePrecious Time

Read more at www.wjmaybooks.com.

Daughter of Darkness - Victoria - Box Set

Fae Wilds Series
Twist and Turns
Curse of the Fae
Force the Truth

Great Temptation Series
The Devil's Footsteps
Heaven's Command
Mortals Surrender

Hidden Secrets Saga
Seventh Mark - Part 1
Seventh Mark - Part 2
Marked By Destiny
Compelled
Fate's Intervention
Chosen Three
The Hidden Secrets Saga: The Complete Series

Kerrigan Chronicles
Stopping Time
A Passage of Time
Ticking Clock
Secrets in Time

Time in the City
Ultimate Future

Kerrigan Memoirs
Chronicles of Devon
Chronicles of Angel
Chronicles of Julian
Chronicles of Molly
Chronicles of Gabriel
Chronicles of Rae

Kerrigan Presidents Series
Leaders in Control

Mending Magic Series
Lost Souls
Illusion of Power
Challenging the Dark
Castle of Power
Limits of Magic
Protectors of Light
Mending Magic Box Set Books #1-3

Omega Queen Series
Discipline
Bravery

Courage
Conquer
Strength
Validation
Approval
Blessing
Balance
Grievance
Enchanted
Gratified
Omega Queen - Box Set Books #1-3

Paranormal Huntress Series
Never Look Back
Coven Master
Alpha's Permission
Blood Bonding
Oracle of Nightmares
Shadows in the Night
Paranormal Huntress BOX SET

Prophecy Series
Only the Beginning
White Winter
Secrets of Destiny

Revamped Series
Hidden

Strength & Power
Last One Standing
Rae of Light
The Chronicles of Kerrigan Box Set Books # 1 - 6

The Chronicles of Kerrigan: Gabriel
Living in the Past
Present For Today
Staring at the Future

The Chronicles of Kerrigan Prequel
Christmas Before the Magic
Question the Darkness
Into the Darkness
Fight the Darkness
Alone in the Darkness
Lost in Darkness
The Chronicles of Kerrigan Prequel Series Books #1-3

The Chronicles of Kerrigan Sequel
A Matter of Time
Time Piece
Second Chance
Glitch in Time
Our Time
Precious Time

The Hidden Secrets Saga
Seventh Mark (part 1 & 2)

The Kerrigan Kids
School of Potential
Myths & Magic
Kith & Kin
Playing With Power
Line of Ancestry
Descent of Hope
Illusion of Shadows
Frozen by the Future
Guilt Of My Past
Demise of Magic
Rise of The Prophecy
Deafened By The Past
The Kerrigan Kids Box Set Books #1-3

The Queen's Alpha Series
Eternal
Everlasting
Unceasing
Evermore
Forever
Boundless
Prophecy
Protected
Foretelling

Revelation
Betrayal
Resolved
The Queen's Alpha Box Set

The Senseless Series
Radium Halos - Part 1
Radium Halos - Part 2
Nonsense
Perception
The Senseless - Box Set Books #1-4

Standalone
Shadow of Doubt (Part 1 & 2)
Five Shades of Fantasy
Zwarte Nevel
Shadow of Doubt - Part 1
Shadow of Doubt - Part 2
Four and a Half Shades of Fantasy
Dream Fighter
What Creeps in the Night
Forest of the Forbidden
Arcane Forest: A Fantasy Anthology
The First Fantasy Box Set

Watch for more at www.wjmaybooks.com.

About the Author

About W.J. May

Welcome to USA TODAY BESTSELLING author W.J. May's Page! SIGN UP for W.J. May's Newsletter to find out about new releases, updates, cover reveals and even freebies! http://eepurl.com/97aYf

Website: http://www.wjmaybooks.com

Facebook: http://www.facebook.com/pages/Author-WJ-May-FAN-PAGE/141170442608149?ref=hl *Please feel free to connect with me and share your comments. I love connecting with my readers.* W.J. May grew up in the fruit belt of Ontario. Crazy-happy childhood, she always has had a vivid imagination and loads of energy. After her father passed away in 2008, from a six-year battle with cancer (which she still believes he won the fight against), she began to write again. A passion she'd loved for years, but realized life was too short to keep putting it off. She is a writer of Young Adult, Fantasy Fiction and where ever else her little muses take her.

Read more at www.wjmaybooks.com.

www.ingramcontent.com/pod-product-compliance
Lightning Source LLC
Chambersburg PA
CBHW061514120726
48001CB00004B/1320